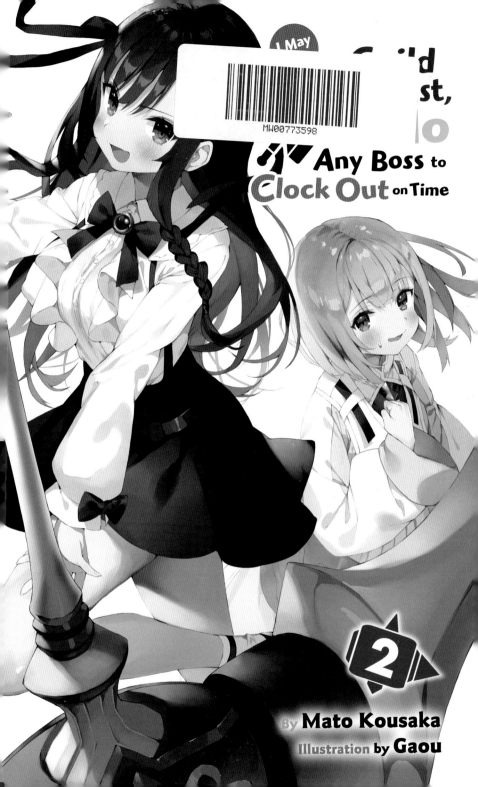

I May Be a Guild Receptionist, but I'll Solo Any Boss to Clock Out on Time

Characters

CHARACTER 1
Alina Clover

A girl working her dream job as a receptionist. Completely uninterested in aiming high, she's satisfied with the stability and security of her current career. But if this exhausting overtime keeps up, her hidden side might show...

CHARACTER 2
The Executioner

A powerful adventurer who is the subject of many rumors. Whenever adventurers are stuck on a dungeon, they'll swoop in, solo the boss, and leave without a word. Some say they have to be a total hottie, but it's not even clear if they exist.

CHARACTER 3
Jade Scrade

The leader and tank of Silver Sword, the strongest party in the guild. He's a good-looking and sincere man of few words, which has earned him a lot of fans. After learning Alina's secret, he does everything he can to get her to join his party, but...

CHARACTER 4
Lululee Ashford

Silver Sword's healer. Despite her youthful appearance, she's a member of the strongest party in the guild. Possesses a rare skill and healing magic.

CHARACTER 5
Lowe Losblender

Silver Sword's ranged attacker. The life of his party. As a black mage, he specializes in powerful attack magic.

CHARACTER 6
Laila

The newest receptionist at Iffole Counter. She's a total fangirl for the Executioner and obsesses over their (presumably) handsome looks.

CHARACTER 7
Glen Garia

Guildmaster of the Iffole Adventurers Guild. In his youth, he was a highly capable frontline attacker and member of Silver Sword.

The Centennial Festival

A large festival the city of Iffole puts on every year. It was originally held to emulate the ceremonies of the "ancients," the people who once lived on the continent of Helcacia, but it's expanded in scope every year since then. Today, the event is one of Iffole's biggest draws and lasts for three days and three nights, attracting vendors and entertainers from far and wide.

I May Be a Guild Receptionist, but I'll Solo Any Boss to Clock Out on Time

Mato Kousaka

Illustration by Gaou

YEN ON

NEW YORK

Mato Kousaka

Translation by Jennifer Ward
Cover art by Gaou
. . . .

GUILD NO UKETSUKEJO DESUGA,
ZANGYO WA IYANANODE BOSS O SOLO TOBATSUSHIYO TO OMOIMASU Vol.2
©Mato Kousaka 2021
Edited by Dengeki Bunko
First published in Japan in 2021 by KADOKAWA CORPORATION, Tokyo.
English translation rights arranged with KADOKAWA CORPORATION, Tokyo,
through TUTTLE-MORI AGENCY, INC., Tokyo.

English translation © 2024 by Yen Press, LLC

Yen On
150 West 30th Street, 19th Floor
New York, NY 10001

Visit us at yenpress.com • facebook.com/yenpress • twitter.com/yenpress
yenpress.tumblr.com • instagram.com/yenpress

First Yen On Edition: January 2024
Edited by Yen On Editorial: Maya Deutsch
Designed by Yen Press Design: Madelaine Norman

Yen On is an imprint of Yen Press, LLC.
The Yen On name and logo are trademarks of Yen Press, LLC.

The publisher is not responsible for websites (or their content) that are not owned by the publisher.

Library of Congress Cataloging-in-Publication Data
Names: Kousaka, Mato, author. | Gaou, illustrator. | Ward, Jennifer (Jennifer J.), translator.
Title: I may be a guild receptionist, but I'll solo any boss to clock out on time / Mato Kousaka ; illustration by Gaou ; translated by Jennifer Ward.
Other titles: Guild no uketsukejou desu ga, zangyou wa Iya nanode boss wo solo toubatsu shiyou to omoimasu. English
Description: First Yen On edition. | New York, NY : Yen On, 2023–
Identifiers: LCCN 2023022303 | ISBN 9781975369460 (v. 1 ; trade paperback) |
   ISBN 9781975369484 (v. 2 ; trade paperback) | ISBN 9781975369507 (v. 3 ; trade paperback) |
   ISBN 9781975369521 (v. 4 ; trade paperback)
Subjects: CYAC: Adventure and adventurers—Fiction. | Monsters—Fiction. | LCGFT: Action and adventure fiction. | Monster fiction. | Light novels.
Classification: LCC PZ7.1.K684 Id 2023 | DDC [Fic]—dc23
LC record available at https://lccn.loc.gov/2023022303

ISBNs: 978-1-9753-6948-4 (paperback)
         978-1-9753-6949-1 (ebook)

10 9 8 7 6 5 4 3 2 1

LSC-C

Printed in the United States of America

1

People used to always call me slow and stupid.

I was bad at my studies. I was bad at sports.

I was worse than everyone else, and sluggish to catch on, no matter what I did.

But even I wanted people to rely on me. No—it was because I couldn't do anything that I wanted to believe I could find my worth by being needed. I wanted to feel confident in myself.

That was why I became a healer, since the work they do is inherently valuable. They're sought after.

I was okay with just firing heals from the shadow of the tank.

I may have been slow and stupid, but I wouldn't cause trouble for anyone if I hid behind the muscle of my party.

The job was simple, safe, and would always be in demand.

There's no better role for me, I thought.

Even I can do this.

I was so dishonest.

I hid behind the image of a purehearted healer, someone who showed consideration for others and comforted her allies...even though I was utterly crafty and craven on the inside.

I'd taken up the profession out of these twisted ulterior motives, without really being prepared for what it entailed.

That was why my party members died.

2

It was Alina's third year as a receptionist at the Adventurers Guild.

She hadn't been working there long enough to call herself a veteran, but she was past being a newbie at this point and had grown familiar with the job.

Alina had set a goal for herself recently. It was very, *very* important that she actualized it, even if it meant risking her life.

"Good luck out there!"

Standing at the quest counter, she saw off the adventurer who had finished registering for their quest with a smile.

When her reception window was busy, she would put off the processing done on the quest forms, but now she had the time to quickly get it done on the spot. When that was finished, she carefully checked to make sure she had filled out everything, then laid the form on the stack.

"Ahh, it's so peaceful…!" Alina muttered with satisfaction.

She worked at Iffole Counter, the largest quest-processing facility in the great city of Iffole.

Standing at one of the five reception windows at the office, Alina swept her gaze to the opposite side of the reception area.

Soft sunlight shone in through the skylight up above as the adventurers looking at the quest board, which spanned an entire wall, calmly selected their quests. The clock had just struck twelve, signifying that Alina's lunch break had arrived. The morning part of her shift was about to wind down.

"All right, it's time for lunch!"

Right as the afternoon bell rang on the city clock tower, Alina stretched and groaned. The receptionists standing at the other windows all headed for their lunch breaks one after another. Alina put up a note reading MORNING RECEPTION HOURS ARE OVER and started to leave in high spirits.

That was when it happened.

"Hold on, hold on, hold on!" a large-framed adventurer yelled as he dashed into Iffole Counter.

Aline froze in place, caught off guard for an instant—that would be her downfall.

That adventurer didn't even look at any of the other reception windows, immediately fixing his eyes on Alina and practically leaping over to her counter.

"Safe! I got here before the morning ended!"

Uh, you definitely didn't...

It was true that Alina was still standing behind the counter, but there was no question that the morning reception period had elapsed.

But the adventurer breathed a sigh of relief for some reason, like he was thinking, *As far as I'm concerned, it's still morning out there.* He then wiped off his sweat and said, entirely shamelessly, "There's a quest I'm in a bit of a rush to sign up for. I know I can't register during lunch, but I figured I'd be okay if I came up to your window, even if it was a little past time, so I dashed right over! Yeah, what a relief! Go on, register me, please!"

Yeah, you can just drop dead.

Alina nearly let her thoughts escape from behind her frozen smile. Though she just barely held herself back, she was overcome with an intense desire to kill now that she'd learned the man's crime was premeditated.

He was pulling this nonsense so casually, thinking he would just take twenty minutes of her time or so. Frankly speaking, this was a grave offense.

Her break was an integral reprieve from her long workday. It was a heavenly hour, during which she could escape from irritating relationships and liberate her spirit. She couldn't waste a minute—no, even a second—of that time, and yet this man had the nerve to tell her to give some of it up. She couldn't allow this.

"…"

But all Alina could do was feel regret.

The man clearly hadn't made it to the counter in time. But did that mean she was unable to offer him service? Not at all. He couldn't have barged in at a worse time. If only she hadn't frozen up—then she could have at least claimed that she didn't notice him.

"…Yes, it's still all right. Please select the quest you wish to accept."

She would have liked to spend about an hour beating into this adventurer just how much goodwill, how much sacrifice it had taken on her part to say that to him. But Alina swallowed it all down and flashed him her plastered-on smile.

In situations like these, brushing clients off out of hand was bound to lead to complaints down the line. After weighing the slight inconvenience of losing some of her lunch break against the risk of being forced to write complaint forms and multiplying her workload, Alina chose the former and accepted her fate.

She could tell at a glance that this guy was a regular who often lined up at her reception window. Shoving his face into her mental blacklist, Alina told herself that this was all part of the job, her lips trembling slightly.

The objective she had sworn to accomplish popped up in the back of her mind.

Yes, I have my goal. I can't be stupid and add unnecessary work for myself—

****

"What a disaster this afternoon, huh, Alina?"

Alina heard a voice as she took her late lunch break at her desk.

It belonged to a charming girl who had impressively large dark eyes and swaying pigtails. Her name was Laila, a new receptionist two years Alina's junior who had started working at Iffole Counter this year.

"...It really was... Augh..." Sulking childishly, Alina stuffed her cheeks with the pastry she'd brought for lunch like she was taking revenge.

There had been a few snags during the registration process, and Alina wound up spending half her lunch break helping the man sign up for the quest. While she typically took her lunches outside, she didn't have the time for that today, so she resigned herself to eating at her desk.

"Why is it that the people who come at the last minute always have some major issue...? Especially when the load has been so light at the counter lately... Why do I have to work on my lunch break when it isn't even busy...?!"

Laila widened her eyes in surprise as she watched a dark, murderous aura develop around her colleague. "Alina, you really look awful when you're angry...! You're so pretty when you aren't ranting about something, so drop the monster face! Otherwise, you'll turn off all the men in the world...!"

"I don't care whether I'm beauty or the beast; it's my right to be mad about the sanctity of my lunch break getting defiled."

Alina chewed the last of her pastry and swallowed it, then lifted her head with eyes ablaze.

Her good looks had won her a modest following among her clientele.

She had long, glossy black hair; large, charming jade eyes; soft fine skin; and a delicate frame. If she just knew when to keep her mouth shut, then this lovely girl of seventeen would have stolen hearts.

But now that her expression was one of unconcealed hatred—her pink lips twisted up, and her charming jade eyes flashing with the urge to kill—Alina looked utterly imposing. Her beauty was completely tarnished.

"Those damn adventurers, eating up my lunch break…! They won't live this down…! They deserve death…!"

"Why do I even bother saying anything to you…?" Laila gave up and sighed as she looked at Alina, whose beautiful face was a mask of unconcealed rage. "Anyway, couldn't you have just told that guy to come back later?"

"I wanted to avoid even the smallest chance of getting saddled with more busywork." Alina clenched her fist with a *hmph*. "I'll do whatever it takes to accomplish my goal this year…!"

"You goal…?"

Alina glared at a leaflet that was posted on the wall.

Her tired eyes were bloodshot from being flared wide in anger through all the extra work she'd done, and they had taken on a sort of ghastly vigor.

Widening them even further, Alina cried, "The Centennial Festival!!"

A variety of advertisements were posted on the wall of Iffole Counter since it got a lot of foot traffic. And one of those was a flyer for an event that would be held a week from now.

The Centennial Festival.

It was the largest event of its kind in the city of Iffole. It had been started to imitate and research the rituals of the ancients, who once lived on the continent of Helcacia. These days, however, it was mainly an excuse for adventurers to throw a wild party.

The Centennial Festival got wilder every year, and it had grown to the point where it was one of Iffole's main attractions. Spanning three days and three nights, it drew in visitors from far and wide. And since crowds of people were excellent business opportunities, skilled chefs, merchants, and even entertainers also traveled to Iffole to set up stalls on the streets.

Suffice it to say, no one was the least bit concerned with imitating

the solemn ceremony—a ritual for entreating the power of Dia—
that the ancients were said to have once carried to this land. It had
become one large event for drinking and partying.

With the Centennial Festival drawing near, it felt like the whole
city was astir. Feeling the restless energy, Alina clenched her
fists as she expressed the frustration in her heart. "Last year and
the year before that, I had so much overtime that I couldn't go to
the festival…! Do you know how hard it was working by myself as I
heard people outside having fun…?! It was practically torture…!"

"Ahh…of course… I don't really want to imagine it…"

"But this year, it'll happen for sure! I'm going to leave work on
time and go to the Centennial Festival or die trying!"

Alina jabbed her feather pen into the air, staring into the heavens
like a god of war leading her soldiers to charge onto the battlefield.
Nay—Alina's determination to achieve her objective was just that
strong.

"And I'm going to live it up for three days and three nights!!"

Yes—this was Alina's greatest aspiration now that she'd entered
her third year as a receptionist.

After all, could there have been anything more foolish than living in Iffole for three years without enjoying the festivities even
once? No, there was not. She would be there this year, whatever it
took. She had to.

Even if she had to exchange her labor and time for money to
support her lifestyle, people all had the right to enjoy the things
they loved. Alina could use her time however she pleased. It wasn't
fair in the slightest to have that right crushed by the cruelty of
overtime.

At this point, her objective went beyond something as trite as
wanting to go to the festival because she was sick of working late.
This was a laborer's war to regain her dignity as a human being—
she was winning back her freedom…!

"I'm looking forward to the Centennial Festival, too!" Alina's passion made Laila's eyes sparkle, too. "The biggest event in Iffole! You know, one of the reasons I wanted to be a receptionist in Iffole was that if I lived here, then I could enjoy the Centennial Festival every year!"

But then Laila tilted her head with a *huh? But wait*, as if she had just realized something. "Do you need to get yourself this hyped up to be able to leave on time on the day of the Centennial Festival…? We haven't had any overtime lately, so at this rate, we can just zip through to finish up work, right? Since we're receptionists."

"I understand what you're trying to say, Laila."

Receptionists were public servants who processed quests, registered adventurers, and kindly sent people off to explore dangerous dungeons.

People called reception work a lifetime position since it was stable and difficult to get fired from. Unlike adventuring, it didn't require you to risk your life, came with a lot of social trust, and guaranteed you a salary for life. It was the ideal career—provided you could put on forced smiles for filthy, arrogant adventurers and dispassionately carry out the most stupidly unfulfilling office work in their service. Generally, however, it was a job where you could take it easy.

"But that's a naive thought—and a very foolish one," Alina continued.

"Huh?"

"This place turns into a war zone on the day of the Centennial Festival."

"What?!" Laila widened her eyes in shock.

In a cold tone filled with many years of resentment, Alina elaborated. "It's all because of that damn Centennial Festival Special Bonus Period, when quests taken during the festivities receive a bonus on top of their usual completion rewards…"

"Sp-special bonus period?!" Laila staggered in place, as though she had been struck by lightning. "Hold on a minute, please—there's a bonus on completion rewards?! What the heck?! No one told me about this!"

"Guild headquarters sent us the notice about it just the other day. The more important something is, the more they drag their feet warning you about it. You've got to be responsible and check these things for yourself to prepare, or you'll get taken by surprise and stabbed in the back."

In her first year as a receptionist, Alina had also totally missed the notice and totally been stabbed in the back. It had been the death of her. But now that Laila was committing the same error, Alina could lecture her smugly.

"Adventurers who have been holding their breath waiting for the special bonus period will band together and storm the reception counter to take quests once it starts... You get what that means, don't you? There's going to be *a ton* of paperwork to get through during office hours while the Centennial Festival is running. You'll be getting home *very* late. And when things get like that, all that awaits you is death."

"Death...!"

"I've always been so busy with overtime during the Centennial Festival that I never had time to enjoy it...!"

Though receptionists typically had regular hours, when certain conditions lined up, they suddenly found themselves drowning in a pool of hellish overtime.

That would happen when a new dungeon was discovered or a dungeon was right about to be completed—or at times like now, when the guild got in the mood to make an event of things and implement a limited bonus on completion rewards. In those situations, hordes of adventurers, eyes blinded by greed, would come surging in. They would take quests like people possessed and create a mountain of overtime for the receptionists.

Things got so busy during these periods of extra work that minimum standards for a healthy lifestyle would fall by the wayside.

You'd do everything you could to tackle your overtime, and by the time you crawled back home and threw down whatever miserable excuse for a meal you made with the little energy you had left, you'd be too exhausted to do anything but sleep... Of course, by the time you had the stamina to go to the festival, it would already be over.

"The guild's filthy decision to increase quest rewards during the Centennial Festival left me defeated every year... I could never handle the massive amount of office work. I had so much overtime that I couldn't attend the festivities...!"

"Filthy?"

"It must be so nice being an adventurer who has nothing to worry about... They just have to get the application in during the bonus period to get the extra rewards, so they can enjoy the festival while it's happening, then take their time finishing the quest after it's over—they get to have their cake and eat it, too... No wonder they come crawling out from under everything..."

"Alina...that look in your eyes is scaring me..."

"Take a gander at this."

Alina's intensity was making her junior tremble, but she ignored that and smacked a stack of papers on the desk. On the cover, in bombastic style, was written CENTENNIAL FESTIVAL SPECIAL BONUS PERIOD ULTIMATE STRATEGY GUIDE.

"Wh-what is this...?!"

"This manual is a record of trends and tactics for handling the quest rush during the Centennial Festival bonus period... I'm not gonna be stuck drowning in overtime forever. More importantly—!"

Alina spread open a booklet that she had carefully placed at the side of her desk.

It was a guidebook packed with details about the Centennial Festival for tourists. While it was small enough to carry on your person, it was somewhat thick and featured information on what was happening on each day of the festival, street stall locations, and exciting illustrations. These were supposed to be handed out to people attending the festival from outside Iffole, but Alina had gotten her hands on it as soon as she could and had already added some little notes to it.

"I've memorized the official schedule that was issued by the Centennial Festival Committee, and thanks to my thorough information gathering, I've already got a handle on the locations of popular stalls whose products are going to sell out. I've already selected which I want to swing by and have calculated three different optimally efficient pathways to cover everything…! Now I just have to avoid overtime and leave on time during the three days of the Centennial Festival…!"

"W-wow… You're even more jazzed about the festival this year because you were too busy to attend before, huh…"

"Heh-heh…heh-heh-heh-heh-heh-heh… Just you wait, Centennial Festival…! Things'll be different now that I'm armed with the techniques I've built during my three years as a receptionist…! I'm going to go home on time and enjoy the hell out of the Centennial Festival this year, nooooo matter *what*…!"

With a tremendous sort of passion for the Centennial Festival and blazing with dark flames, Alina clenched her fists.

3

"Oh, it's so great to leave work on time…" Alina's cheery voice was absorbed into the streets of Iffole.

Just like remembering to be thankful for your food, it was important to digest the joy of being able to leave work on time on days when you could. Only those who had experienced the hell of overtime could understand this joy.

The people of Iffole were done with work and were returning home. Alina left Iffole Counter to mingle with the crowd and head on home—but no, she had a bit of a side trip first.

"Hello!" With that cheery greeting, she walked into her favorite business. It was a cozy brickwork shop that featured rows of refrigerated cases powered by relic technology with rows of various cakes inside.

"This one, and this one, and this one, and this one too, please." After buying a whole bunch of cakes, Alina headed home, a smirk on her face.

She'd just bought an armful of cakes on the way home from work. Only a working adult was allowed this kind of luxury. Most importantly, she'd been able to get off work early enough that the shop was still open!

"Leaving work on time is such a privilege. I feel like a winner…!!"

She could have cake for dinner when she had overtime, but then it wouldn't taste good at all. But going back to home sweet home on schedule and devouring her sweets alone—that was one of Alina's top evening activities.

"Gonna head home and eat lots of cake!"

As Alina hummed along, her gaze wandered to the center of a large city square.

It was a flagstone-paved piazza in the center of Iffole. The square was rather pretty, with a giant blue crystal gate and a fountain, but it was a little more cluttered than usual now, since people were setting things up for the Centennial Festival, which was a month away.

There was a pile of lumber in the square, and the water fountain had been turned off and covered with a tarp.

This square would be unveiled on the final day of the Centennial Festival, on the night when the festival enthusiasm had reached its peak.

Alina would not brag about this (she really wouldn't), but she'd

gotten through many, many brushes with overtime. After each period of crunch, she'd been able to get through her office work faster and make fewer errors. She felt like she'd grown a lot as a receptionist lately.

I can do it…! This year for sure, I know I can do it…!

She'd been made to drink her tears for the last two Centennial Festivals. But this time around, she would surely make up for her losses and—

Just as she was starting to overflow with determination, an excited voice brought her to a stop. "Alina!"

An adventurer was rushing up to her, all charming smiles.

He was a young man with the kind of handsome face that would make you do a double take if you passed him on the street. He stood a head taller than the average person, and his strong and firm frame was tucked in light armor, which swayed slightly from the giant shield on his back. Women couldn't help but turn to look at him when they were in his vicinity, and those who recognized him would even shriek with glee when they saw him.

"…"

That very man was racing toward Alina, with eyes for no one else, but her expression was just as severe as always. No, it was worse—an intense wrinkle had formed between her brows.

"What?" The question escaped her lips in a low tone.

After running to her side, Jade stopped and eyed the scowling receptionist wordlessly for a while. Eventually, he gave a little sigh, and voice trembling with emotion, he said, "Ahh…I'm absorbing my Alina quotient for the first time in a month…!"

"Can you stop talking like a creep?"

Nobody living in Iffole would fail to recognize the man who had appeared—for he was Jade Scrade, renowned as the strongest adventurer in the guild.

The setting sun lit his silver hair, his face beloved by the gods, and his blessed physique. But Jade was more than looks. People called him the strongest tank in the guild, and for good reason: He was the first person in adventurer history to have manifested three Sigurth skills, a class of ability that most people were lucky to have one of. This prodigy was a member of Silver Sword, an elite party of powerful and select adventurers, and he'd been entrusted to lead them at just nineteen.

But contrary to his spectacular appearance, Jade was also a serial stalker. He'd pursued Alina relentlessly ever since she'd caught his eye, no matter if she hit or insulted him. And on top of that, even after nearly losing his life, he had demonstrated the vitality of a cockroach, crawling back from the brink of death to keep bothering her. The man was like a zombie.

"On your way back from work, Alina?" Jade asked.

"I know you know that because you were sneaking around watching."

"Yeah. That's what I came for!"

"Agh, I see…" Not only did he readily acknowledge his behavior, but he was even weirdly proud of it, making Alina scowl.

But as she cursed him about a hundred times in her head, Jade started muttering on about something. "Anyway, Alina. Somewhere in my heart, I kind of believed…that you might come visit me while I was recovering, at some point…at least once."

"…"

Alina shifted her gaze to the side at the way he deliberately emphasized the word *visit*. Meanwhile, Jade slumped, as he said in a clearly sad voice, "You were so blatant about it. You didn't even come a *siiiiiingle* time…"

"Why would I come visit you?"

"I was using my Sigurth skill the whole time, checking to see if you were nearby…"

"Just shut up and rest."

"But even then, I never sensed you…"

"Well, yeah, I never went anywhere near you, so that's a given."

"But we're comrades! We got through that deadly crisis together!!"

"It was just coincidence that we happened to fight side by side."

"No way…!"

"And wait, weren't you supposed to spend three months at home recovering? It still hasn't even been a month."

Yes, it was strange that Jade was here right now, wailing at her with so much vigor. From what she'd heard a month ago, he had been hurt so badly that it would take him three months to make a full recovery, so he'd been told to refrain from adventuring and rest at home.

Thanks to that, the last month had been truly peaceful. Alina hadn't been stalked or ambushed after work, and she'd been able to enjoy her time alone.

So then why was this "Creepy silver cockroach already running free?"

"You said that last part of your thought out loud, Alina."

"Because it's what I think."

"Heh-heh-heh. I'm so healthy that I recover from most wounds in a month."

"I see…"

There was no way that could be true, but since it would be a hassle to interrogate him any further, Alina dropped things there and sighed, then went into an empty back alley. Jade was a complete stalker on the inside, but he was essentially an elite leader who was equal in status to the people who ran the guild. He drew too much attention, in more ways than one. A mere receptionist like Alina shouldn't have been insulting a guy like him on the street to begin with.

Though Jade had been openly showing his affection for Alina so frequently as of late that the townspeople around them were actually pretending not to notice out of consideration.

Following Alina into the back alley, Jade suddenly changed the subject. "More importantly, have you considered what we talked about?"

"What was that again?"

"Isn't it obvious?! I mean you joining Silver Sword!" Eyes blazing, Jade jabbed at her with his index finger. "A month ago, you fought a deadly battle against a terrible foe—a dark god—together with us as a member of Silver Sword! I was thinking that would have given you an understanding of what being an adventurer is like and convince you to join us."

"I'm not interested," Alina shot back as she dispassionately kept walking.

"With your powers, becoming an adventurer and a billionaire isn't just a dream, you know?"

"My dream isn't to become a billionaire; it's to live an *uneventful* life as a receptionist! And for starters, I only did that last month because you promised that you would increase the number of staff at Iffole Counter and get rid of my overtime! Could you leave me alone forever?"

"Ngh…well, I thought you might say that." Still not giving up, Jade groaned, then rummaged through his belongings to pull out a piece of paper. "Which is why I brought you a compromise today."

"A compromise?"

"I've had nothing to do for a whole month. So the whole time, I've been thinking of a way you could be a receptionist while also joining Silver Sword. If we do this, it'll take care of everything—look!"

"Wha…?"

Alina froze as she examined the piece of paper Jade had shoved in her face.

There, spelled out in dramatic characters, was the following: *By the order of Silver Sword representative Jade Scrade, I appoint Alina Clover as Silver Sword's exclusive receptionist.*

"What...is...this?" Alina read over the comment in blank amazement; it had even been stamped with the official guild seal.

Jade curled his lips in elation. "As the leader of Silver Sword, I have the right to appoint an exclusive receptionist to our party. I spoke directly with the guildmaster and forced him to— Ahhhhh, don't rip that up!!"

No sooner had he thrust the document at Alina than she had expressionlessly yanked it away and ripped it into four pieces without hesitation. Jade panicked out of the corner of her eye as she balled it up and threw it away. "Don't give me this crap, you stalking cockroach bastard..."

"Cockroach?!"

"If I became your party's exclusive receptionist, I would have quests dropping in on me day and night!! I would have no days off and no room to live my life!! It would be a totally exploitative work environment!!!" Alina cried.

Jade's expression stiffened awkwardly. "...N-no, that's not true."

"Just you try and make me Silver Sword's exclusive receptionist with that power of yours... I'll tenderize you so hard with my hammer that you'll be unrecognizable. I'll make you regret being born...," Alina muttered darkly, then summoned a giant war hammer from thin air.

This was her skill: *Dia Break*.

Dia was the strongest class skill, which currently only Alina possessed. The power was apparently of the same rank as that of the ancients who had once inhabited this land, the people who had built a nation so sophisticated they had called it Diania.

But Alina's story wasn't nearly as fancy. They said that the ancients had received power as blessings from beings revered as Dia, but Alina had manifested *Dia Break* as a result of being exhausted from overtime.

At any rate, there were lots of amazing things about this ability, but right now, Alina had activated it purely for the sake of beating the stalking bastard in front of her to death.

As Alina clutched the war hammer, her voice trembling with rage, Jade panicked and zipped away. But even then, he couldn't let his proposal go, shouting, "Y-y-y-you know, if I use my authority! I can do something about your personnel situation!"

Alina raised a brow at his remark. "...Uh-huh. So you'll go that far, huh? I can tell you're reaaaaal serious."

"Really?! Then you'll join Silver Swo— Bwah!!"

For an instant, Jade's face was sparkling gladly—then in the next moment, Alina's war hammer was slamming right into his cheek. Jade was hurled away, going into a tailspin before sliding along the ground, crashing into an alley wall, and finally coming to a stop.

"Authority, my ass... My life as a receptionist is in danger here...!"

"Hey...wait...my wounds only just healed, and now they're—"

"You need to learn when to give up, you stupid silver bastaaaaaaaaaard!"

"Gyaaaaaaagh!"

When Alina swung around her war hammer, Jade shrieked and ran off. Then a terrific smacking noise followed, and the scream of a young man rang out through the peaceful evening in the city of Iffole.

4

The next morning, at Iffole Counter before reception hours.

Alina and Laila went around wiping down the windows and benches of the guest area, which was hushed without their bosses or seniors around. This was the fate of the underling: cleaning the workplace early in the morning.

"All right, time for another day of hard work! It's all for the Centennial Festival!"

"You're sure fired up about this, Alina."

A meaningful smile came to Laila's face as she noticed Alina's unusual energy. "It's a relief to see you so cheerful, in more ways than one!"

"Heh. Of course I'm cheerful. Since I'm absolutely going to enjoy the Centennial Festival this year, for sure."

Now Alina had a goal to work toward: participating in the Centennial Festival.

Squeezing her eyes tight, she pictured the wondrous scene to come a few days from now. She imagined herself going around amid the backdrop of the bustling sounds of the festival, visiting street stalls of all kinds, eating her fill of delicious foods, buying unusual items from all over the land, drinking good booze, and enjoying things until midnight. Just picturing it made endless strength well up within her. How wonderful the Centennial Festival was...

"Don't you feel like we've gotten more people coming in for quests lately, Alina?"

Alina stiffened as Laila's offhand remark ripped her from her Centennial Festival reverie.

"Things are uneventful as usual, but I guess I'd say the customers are slow but consistent? It's rather strange when it's not even time yet for the Centennial Festival Special Bonus Period, don't you think?" Laila tilted her head with a puzzled look.

"...Yeah, you're right," Alina muttered indistinctly beside her.

Alina had clearly sensed this thing Laila was wondering about, too. Not just sensed it, in fact—since Alina was tasked with totaling the daily number of quests at Iffole Counter, she had the hard numbers to confirm that there were indeed more quests being taken now than at the same time last year.

"I wonder why that is?" Laila wondered aloud.

But Alina chose not to reply and played dumb.

That was because she knew the cause of that minor abnormality was ultimately herself.

But despite Alina's efforts to feign ignorance, Laila guessed at the right answer. "I wonder if this is because of how they found a secret quest a month back..."

"...Yeah...maybe..."

Adventurers took on a variety of quests, from personal favors to clearing dungeons. Those quests were collected by the Adventurers Guild and put up on display, without exception.

Secret quests were another thing entirely—missions that even the Adventurers Guild was unaware of.

These quests had been the subject of urban legend for a long time, and adventurers had embellished their allure over the years by suggesting that accepting one could reveal hidden dungeons or give you access to special relics. Still, secret quests were ultimately nothing but rumors—or at least they had been, until one month ago.

"But to think that a secret quest would be hidden inside a relic! Isn't that amazing?!" Laila cast aside her doubts, her eyes sparkling with blatant curiosity. "I wonder who on earth found it? Relics are made of the hardest substances around, aren't they? You'd have to be insanely strong to destroy one!"

"I guess, yeah... I wonder who did it?" Alina answered briefly as she turned away, in a bit of a cold sweat.

She had done it.

One month ago, Alina destroyed a relic by accident and wound up finding the secret quest hidden inside. And just as the legends said, a hidden dungeon called the White Tower had appeared.

Ostensibly, Silver Sword had been the ones to take on the White Tower and clear it completely, nearly losing their lives in the process. But the truth was that Alina had been deeply involved in that expedition.

Anyway, it was now public knowledge that secret quests were real and that they did indeed lead to hidden dungeons.

Ever since the news broke, adventurers had started retrieving every relic they could get their hands on in an attempt to find more secret quests. Everyone was seeking the "special relics" where hidden dungeons were said to be concealed. That explained the mild increase in the number of quests people were taking lately.

"But, like, the guild has been repeatedly warning everyone about looking for secret quests without due caution because hidden dungeons are so dangerous...," Alina pointed out. "Do all those adventurers have a death wish or what? Even Silver Sword almost bit the dust clearing a hidden dungeon."

"Oh, but that isn't stopping them from looking. If you find a secret quest, you can get the special relic in the hidden dungeon! So basically, that means treasure, right?"

"..."

Relics were the high-tech legacy of the ancients, whose prosperous Helcacian society had been wiped out in a single night.

Now that they were gone, it was nigh impossible to make anything as equivalently advanced as relics—which explained why that lost technology fetched such a high price. For adventurers, they were treasures of unparalleled value.

"And a special treasure, too...! Those relics have to be something incredible if they can't even be compared with gold and silver treasure!"

"Yeah, maybe. I wonder."

"You sound completely unconcerned, Alina."

"Well, I'm not interested."

Despite her statement, Alina knew just what those special relics were.

Gold and silver treasure? The relic they had found was no such thing.

It had taken the form of a human, possessed emotions and intelligence, was capable of speech, fought with a spear, had an incredibly tough body, and wielded multiple Dia skills, laughing as he killed people—also, he had interrupted Alina's overtime. The relic, called a dark god, had been an incredible nuisance. That was what the special relic really was.

The dark god that slumbered in the hidden dungeon had been revived by eating people's souls. He had been such a fearsome foe; he had nearly killed Jade—the strongest tank in the guild—like it was nothing. Worse still, he wasn't the only one; the dark god had said there were more slumbering in this land, making this more than just a minor hassle.

Though Alina had somehow managed to defeat that thing with her Dia skill a month ago, frankly speaking, it had been worse than overtime. It would be horrible if ignorant adventurers found a hidden dungeon and woke up the dark god slumbering within it.

However, information regarding the true nature of these special relics had been completely concealed and hidden from the public out of concern that it would invite confusion. The guildmaster—Glen Garia—had also told Alina not to say a word about the dark gods to anyone.

"M-more importantly! Time for another hard day of work!" Wringing out her rag, Alina changed the subject. "Our fight to attend the Centennial Festival starts now...!"

"That reminds me, I just missed the chance to ask yesterday, but..." Laila stopped cleaning, and no sooner had she turned to Alina questioningly than she'd curled her lips into a smirk. "If you're dead set on going to the Centennial Festival, that must mean—you have a boyfriend!"

"A boyfriend?" Alina blinked in blank surprise. She hadn't been expecting that accusation.

Laila sidled up to her, eyes curved in capricious crescent moons as she jabbed Alina with her elbow. "Awww, come on, Alina, you don't have to play dumb. The Centennial Festival is a super-duper ultra-classic date!"

"What?"

"Huh?"

"I don't know about that."

"But they say that people who go on a date during the Centennial Festival will be together for a hundred years, don't they? That's why some couples even come for the festival from remote villages."

"Huhhh." Since coming to Iffole, Alina had always worked overtime on the day of the Centennial Festival, so there was no way she could have known that. Regardless, she wasn't interested in this information in the slightest, so she dismissed Laila's story. Just as Alina got back to her wiping, Laila grabbed her by the shoulder and drew her back.

"Hey, heyheyheyhey, hold on, please. If you're not going for a date, then who are you planning on going with?"

"Huh? I'm going by myself."

"By yourself?!?!"

"What's the big deal?"

"B-but the Centennial Festival is going to be full of couples…! There'll be people flirting and kissing all over the place! And you're just going to charge right in there? Do you have a death wish?!"

"It's not like the Centennial Festival is just for couples. What's wrong with enjoying it alone?"

"Y…you're so strong…!"

Laila widened her eyes as if she'd been punched, then crumpled on the spot. "So this is…the fate of an overtime master…?!"

"Hey."

"*Hrng…* I'd like to go with you, but unfortunately, I have a date with my special someone…"

"I see."

"Are you curious about him?! You've got to be, right?! You must want to know who your junior is going on a date with!"

"Not really—"

"Tee-hee. Well, don't be *too* shocked when I tell you, Alina."

Laila cut her off, then puffed out her chest and confidently declared, "It's the great Executioner!"

There was a weak *sloop* sound as Alina slipped on a rag and landed dramatically on her face. "*Gack!* I—I hit myself somewhere funny."

"Gosh, you don't have to be *that* surprised!"

"How could I not be?!"

The Executioner was the nickname of a mysterious adventurer who had suddenly become the talk of the town.

They'd gotten their name from the way they would show up in dungeons that the other adventurers had gotten stuck on and curb stomp the floor boss all by themselves.

The Executioner wore an overcoat that concealed their appearance from head to toe, so no one had ever ascertained their identity. They also possessed an unknown skill that allowed them to summon a war hammer, which they would use to beat their foes to a pulp. This last quality had made them an urban legend among adventurers.

No—it was more accurate to say that they *had* been an urban legend.

One month ago, Jade of Silver Sword had testified that the Executioner really existed. This wasn't exactly a surprise—the Executioner had appeared in Iffole shortly before this and defeated a rampaging monster with their immense strength. On top of that, they had also defeated the boss of a hidden dungeon and saved Silver Sword when they'd all been on the verge of being wiped out.

Yes. The Executioner was, in fact, Alina.

Two years ago, Alina abruptly manifested a Dia skill after growing exhausted from all her overtime, then went around defeating the bosses that had been holding things up... But before she knew it, her exploits gave rise to a host of rumors.

A date with the Executioner...? It can't be... Is someone tricking her?!

It was true that Laila could be a little ignorant of the ways of the world and that she was particularly enamored with this mysterious

Executioner. If some guy told Laila that he was the Executioner, Alina could easily see her believing him.

Alina broke into a cold sweat. She had to go about this delicately.

Laila smiled boldly at her. "Heh-heh-heh…I get what you're trying to say. You think there's no way I could have a date with the Executioner, but I can totally make it happen. With this!" she said, enthusiastically revealing a doll that was about the size of her palm.

The doll had a big head that was completely hidden in a coat. Though its face was concealed by its hood, it had an incredibly detailed silver hammer on its back.

Upon realizing that the situation was far less troublesome than she'd envisioned, Alina blinked at Laila in blank surprise. "Is that… an Executioner doll…?"

"What do you think of it?! I've been working on it in the evenings! Now I can have the date of my dreams by going to the festival with my Executioner doll!"

"…Is there a spell on that thing that'll make it turn human or something?"

"Huh? Of course not. A doll is a doll. But please take a good look at it! I got super into all the details. Look, you can take the hood off! And I gave him the super handsome features I imagine him having underneath!" Laila huffed with enthusiasm, leaning toward Alina and pulling off the hood to try and show her.

But Alina restrained her with a sigh. "Yeah, yeah, okay, I get it. I see where you're going with this, so put that thing away."

She really wanted to avoid talking about the Executioner as much as possible, but Laila was totally devoted to the mysterious adventurer, and she gushed about her affection for "him" every chance she got. Once she started talking, she wouldn't stop. It had become a hassle to deal with lately, so Alina would cut her off before she got too into it.

"…" Laila dejectedly put away the doll; evidently, she hadn't gotten what she wanted.

Watching her, Alina balled a fist. "Well, whatever our reasons, there's just one thing we have to do in order to zip out the door the day of the Centennial Festival to enjoy the festivities!"

"That's right!" Having pulled herself together, Laila also thrust out a fist. "I have an exciting date with the Executioner ahead of me, so I have to be totally prepared for the Centennial Festival Special Bonus Pe..." Suddenly, Laila's initial energy dipped, and she trailed off before she could finish her sentence.

"?" Alina gave her a questioning look.

Laila's jaw hung open, and whatever she wanted to say wasn't coming out. Instead, her lips trembled, and her face went white. She stood there frozen in place, her gaze focused on a single point.

"What's wrong?" Alina asked.

"A...Ali...na...look..."

She turned to where Laila was pointing and—

And then she was struck speechless.

"Wha...ha...?"

Her eyes were on the entrance of Iffole Counter. The revolving glass doors had been made using a relic. That in itself wasn't noteworthy, but the sight that lay just outside them was.

Beyond those glass doors, a vast number of adventurers were already crowded in front of the entrance, their eyes flashing like starving beasts as they waited for the minute the doors would open.

"Hey...wha...whaaat?!"

Alina faltered at the sight, and she found herself gritting her teeth and swaying on her feet. She had experienced quest rushes countless times before, but she had never seen one as abnormal as this. Her head turned on its own to the clock on the wall.

Iffole Counter would open in just a few minutes. Once that scant amount of time passed, they would have to open the doors that held back that *herd*. Alina gulped.

She felt like a soldier on the losing side, surrounded by enemy forces.

"A-Alina… What do we do…? What do we do…about that…?"

"Wh-what do we do…? We just have to open up—"

The other older receptionists, who had shown up at the office at some point, were also murmuring to one another about the spectacle.

"Ah! The trays for unprocessed documents…!"

Alina snapped out of it and set out a large number of the "unprocessed" trays that they used during busy periods. They were for tossing in the quest forms adventurers filled out—the receptionists would fill out the necessary sections when the counter was packed, then finish processing them after hours. Alina also set out more quest forms than usual on the counters; she'd switched into "busy" mode.

Meanwhile, Laila timidly unlocked the doors.

"W-welco— Bfft!"

She couldn't even manage to finish her usual greeting before she was tragically buried in the waves of adventurers who poured in. Alina saw that pitiful sight out of the corner of her eye, but she did not have the time to go save her junior, because…

"They're open!"

"Move, I'm first!"

"Shut up, don't push! Back the hell off!"

…the adventurers stormed up to the reception counter in tandem, pushing and jostling with such brutal force that the ground was practically rumbling, their angry roars flying back and forth.

And then all hell broke loose.

5

"…Just what…is going on…?"

Alina's loud question was the only sound in the otherwise hushed Iffole Counter.

Reception hours had ended in the blink of an eye.

The office, illuminated by the crimson light of the setting sun, was in a miserable state.

The quest forms, which should have been placed on the counters, were all over the place; the leaves of the potted plants were torn off and scattered; the benches had been shoved far from their usual positions; and the smaller chairs had been knocked right over.

"What the heck is going on here...?"

Laila was in a similar state of stupefaction, and one of her pigtails had come undone. After locking the door, Alina went limp like her soul had left her body and she slumped over the counter.

She didn't remember much. Honestly, she wasn't even certain if she'd eaten lunch or not. She had been working on pure reflex since she didn't even have the time to process what was going on. Needless to say, the relentless surge of adventurers had kept her from processing a single quest form. The same went for the older receptionists. They were collapsed at their desks in exhaustion and confusion, gazing in a state of shock at the mountain of quest forms they needed to get through, which was more than double the usual height.

"Did the guild implement the bonus earlier than usual...? No, we would have been notified beforehand if they were moving up the extra reward window, and more importantly, the reward amounts haven't changed... A new dungeon hasn't been discovered either, so it's not like there's one that needs clearing... Though I wasn't really focusing on the quests people were taking to begin with..."

Alina was curled up underneath the counter muttering to herself, sorting out the situation bit by bit.

A sudden quest rush generally indicated that a new dungeon had been discovered or a dungeon was on the cusp of being cleared. And even if she hadn't been aware of that information, she would notice everyone taking the same quests during the course of her job and could easily guess the cause—but this time, she was at a loss over the surge of applicants.

"I-it was so sudden... I didn't get why, either..." Even Laila, who loved to gossip and would usually get up to speed on the situation from someone or another, hadn't pinned down the cause this time. "It was so busy that I didn't have the time to chat up the adventurers... And, like, don't you feel like they all looked kind of frenzied...? It was like their eyes were all on fire..."

"When they're acting like that, it means there's some kinda juicy catch dangling in front of them. Adventurers are simpleminded creatures."

"No need to be so nasty about it, Alina."

Somehow getting to their feet, Alina and Laila tidied up the knocked-over bench, the potted plants, and some odds and ends, then both returned to their desks. Alina didn't really want to look straight at it...but her desk area presented a sight even more brutal than the customer space.

Documents had been tossed here and there, and the unprocessed trays were stacked full of forms, some of which were collapsing and causing paper avalanches. They hadn't even had the time to organize things.

"Yeesh...how are there so many...? Is this the work of a monster...?" Laila muttered amid the quiet. The receptionists had exhausted themselves just keeping up with the flood of adventurers while the counter was open, but now they had to fill out all these documents.

Taking in the brutal sight once more, Alina stood there silently for a while. After some time, she pursed her dry lips and muttered, "...Laila, I'm going to go out for a bit."

"Huh?!" Laila widened her eyes in shock at Alina's sudden declaration. "You're going to leave all this behind and go?! But the Centennial Festival...what about our Centennial Festival?!"

"I'm coming back, of course. We're not leaving any work to carry over for the festival...no way! But there's clearly something amiss here. This is beyond just an unexpected rush…! We have to do something, or this year, we'll…"

Be crushed yet again by overtime during the Centennial Festival.

The prospect was so disheartening that Alina couldn't even finish her sentence. But that incomparably cruel possibility felt very real as it weighed down on them.

"…We can't let that happen…!"

She had to know why so many adventurers were signing up for quests. And then she had to nip it in the bud as soon as possible.

Baring her teeth, Alina dashed out of the office.

6

Meanwhile, Jade Scrade was at the training area of the guild headquarters.

Well, it was certainly supposed to be the training facility that had been constructed on the grounds of the guild headquarters, but the scene around him looked nothing like it.

He was in an indoor space supported by four pillars. There weren't any walls, but it felt closed in somehow, and the lighting was dim. The air was damp, as though the place had been closed off for a long time, and the characteristic scent of ether was thick, just like it was in dungeons. The area looked very much like the deepest sections of dungeons, where powerful monsters dwelled—like a boss room.

In the feeble lighting stood a four-legged beast with three heads—a cerberus.

Every time I see it, it's just like the real thing…

Sizing up the cerberus as it growled at him, Jade warily raised his relic arma greatshield.

The monster before them was baring its teeth and ready for battle, yet it wasn't moving to attack. The real thing would have leaped on them long ago, but this one didn't so much as twitch. It was just like a doll.

But that was no surprise. The boss room background and the cerberus were all just visual information—virtual images, a hologram made by a projection machine the guild research team had developed based on a relic.

"Ready anytime! Start," Jade called out, and the cerberus suddenly lifted its head as if life had been breathed into it.

The guild hadn't exactly developed the hologram machine—it was more accurate to say that they had somehow managed to restore a relic that projected three-dimensional data in this manner. The data was stored in a crystal, which the machine would project to create a lifelike image.

But the crystal didn't just record visual information. It worked on all five senses and could read the behavioral patterns and calls of monsters—it even replicated the toughness of their flesh and their attack power. The guild knew nothing, however, about the workings of the technology that made this possible.

That just went to show how incredible the relics of the ancients were.

That explains how they made those dark gods.

At the ready behind Jade were the white mage Lululee, their healer, and the black mage Lowe, their ranged attacker.

And then there was the greatswordsman they had welcomed as their new frontline attacker, a boy named Cybil. At just fifteen, he hadn't been an adventurer long, but even without much experience, he had an exceptional knack for fighting and had taken down giant monsters one after another. This up-and-comer had gained fame with his sword in the blink of an eye.

"Hastor!" Jade chanted, and the light of illusion magic shined from his bared blade. When he thrust the tip into the ground, the cerberus trained all six of its eyes on him.

"Its aggro is on me!"

And with that call from Jade, the battle began.

"Skill Activate: *Sigurth Wall*!" The dark red light of the skill surrounded Jade's shield.

This ability conferred defensive power by hardening its target. A heartbeat later, the cerberus lunged at Jade with speed that belied its large frame, attacking with the sharp claws of its front legs.

Cautiously observing his foe, Jade repelled the strike with his shield.

The cerberus was said to be the guard dog of hell. It was a fearsome foe—strong enough to drive away the regular monsters in A-class dungeons and become a floor boss.

Close in on it, and the creature would lash out with thick limbs and sharp claws; back away from it, and each of its three heads would unleash breath attacks of different elements. Because the cerberus had both the long and short range covered, it was tough to approach. On top of that, it moved fast, leaving hardly any openings to attack. Its whole body was covered in bristly fur that would block nearly all blunt attacks, so slashes were the only physical maneuvers that had an effect on it. That meant Cybil and his greatsword were a good match for the beast.

"Ignis!" Swinging his rod, Lowe activated his attack magic. It was his signature adaptation of a fire spell, a concentrated fireball. The brightly shining orbs exploded before the cerberus's eyes, striking its target's right head and making it sway from impact.

"All right!" Just then, Cybil circled the creature's right flank, swinging his greatsword horizontally and rending the air with a wide strike enhanced by centrifugal force. Making a full-body turn from the waist, he unleashed a powerful blow to the cerberus's most vulnerable spot, lopping off its thick head in a single stroke.

"Yeahhh! How 'bout that! You saw that? Didja just see that?! I got that head in one hit! One hit!!" Cybil cried while taking a step back. Jade smiled wryly at his youthful naivete.

But it was true that Cybil's attack power was worthy of pride. His giant greatsword was attractive—the weapon took all the muscles of his arms and body to handle, and its high attack power practically guaranteed a one-hit kill. But it was difficult to use weapons of that size to their maximum potential against fast foes like the cerberus. While the greatsword appeared to be a simple weapon for people with more muscle than brains, it took a great deal of practice to use properly, and the technique of its wielder greatly affected its attack power.

It would have taken most a while to cut off one of the cerberus's heads, so the fact that Cybil had gotten it in a single strike was proof of his skill.

"Nice, Cybil! On to the next one!"

That being said, this was the point where the fight would get serious.

Graaaaargh!

Now down a head, the cerberus roared even louder.

"Urk!" Cybil struck in the same way he had before, but the cerberus cleanly dodged his blade, skimming Cybil's arms with its claws at the same time. The cerberus's injuries had sent it into a frenzy, nearly doubling its attack power and speed.

The hologram machine determined that Cybil had been hit. A crack was projected onto Cybil's shoulder guard, and there was even holographic blood dripping from his shoulder, splattering onto the floor. Of course, it was just a projection. Cybil didn't have any real injuries to speak of.

"Lululee!" Nevertheless, Jade still shouted an order to their healer, Lululee. Even though this was just training, they couldn't afford to slack off.

"...Heal!" A moment after Jade cried out, a heal spell whizzed by, hitting its mark on Cybil's shoulder.

Huh?

For a moment, Jade sensed that something was off.

Lululee had reacted late. Normally, her spell would be flying by the time Jade gave the order, and her target's wounds would already be patched up.

Is she not focusing because this is just practice...? No, Lululee isn't that kind of person...

But this wasn't the time to worry about a trivial feeling like that.

"Cybil! Once the cerberus gets worked up, it won't flinch like it did before. Be careful!"

"...Roger!"

But now, things were completely different, and Cybil's attacks wouldn't connect because the cerberus was flailing around in agitation.

"Aaaagh! Hit, damn you!"

Cybil was panicking; his movements and attacks were getting desperate, and he was starting to take minor hits here and there. This wasn't a very good trend. If Jade let this keep up, Cybil would eventually take major damage.

If there was one flaw in mock-combat training using the hologram, this was it. Though it simulated injury, that was ultimately just visual information. Since there was no actual pain, people tended to downplay the severity of wounds and not feel the tension that came with a real battle.

What was the right move here? Should they change the flow of battle with Lowe's attack magic? Just as Jade was at a loss over what to do...

A person fell from the ceiling.

"?!"

No—"fell" was putting it lightly. Something plunged into the hologram, swooping in just like a falcon aiming for its prey from high above.

There was a dull crunch as the floor cracked where the individual landed.

They wore a cloak that completely concealed their body and

face. Cybil's eyes widened in shock at the figure's abrupt entrance. "…Huh, is that the Executioner?!"

The Executioner—no, Alina disguised as the Executioner— strode right up to Jade, even though they were right in the middle of a fight with a cerberus.

"There's something I want to ask you," was all she said, her voice low.

"Hey, hold on, Executioner, we're kind of busy right no—"

Graaaaaawr!

Jade's panicked remark was cut off as the agitated cerberus howled at the new presence, throwing the situation into disarray.

"What?" Turning around in annoyance, the Executioner finally noticed the cerberus. There was a monster powerful enough to be a floor boss of an A-class dungeon right in front of her, but not only was she not surprised at its presence, she even clicked her tongue at it. "You're in the way."

Sh-she's…

Her imposing aura told Jade everything he needed to know.

She's really pissed off!!

Jade gasped, then quickly yelled at the invisible research team running the hologram. "C-cancel the training! Take away the cerberus right now!"

But it was too late—too late for the monster, rather.

"Skill Activate: *Dia Break.*" With a quiet chant, the Executioner held up a hand.

Suddenly, a white magical circle glowed at her feet. Faint particles of light gathered in her outstretched hand, and a giant silver war hammer appeared from thin air. It was a beautiful weapon, decorated with intricate silverwork. Opposite the striking end, however, was a section shaped like a pickax—the hammer was as lethal as it was beautiful.

As soon as the Executioner took hold of her hammer, she readied it at the waist and faced the cerberus.

"You're in the way, you stupid muuuuuuuutt!" Screaming with fury that probably had to do with something else, Alina slammed her weapon into the center head with a *thunk*.

The cerberus's cry of pain never arrived.

Instead, a strange crackling sound rang out from the hologram. The uncanny scenery of the boss room rippled in an unstable manner, and the cerberus, which had been thwacked away without a sound, suddenly froze mid-slide on the floor.

"M-measurement failure? It's no good, the hologram is broke— Ahh!"

As the holographic image lost stability, Jade heard the panicked voices of the researchers on the other side of the wall.

Oh dear…

Eventually, there was a grating sound as the whole scene around them vanished, monster and all. Once that dark, cramped scene had cleared, the cold-looking training room and the sprawling sky at sunset became visible.

"………………Huh? One hit?"

Lowering his sword, Cybil looked over at the Executioner in bewilderment. Just the cerberus would be one thing, but her attack had even destroyed the hologram's processing and broken the machine. Now she was staring at her new surroundings in confusion.

Blunt weapons were practically useless in the face of a cerberus's tough hide. You would assume the creature would have resisted the blow of a war hammer because of that, but as was true with anything, resistance didn't mean a thing in the face of overwhelming attack power.

As Cybil stood there speechless, mouth agape, Jade hastily laid a hand on his shoulder. "Cybil, your first attack was good. If you'd continued like that, we would have won. Sorry, but we're calling off the rest of today's training session."

However, it seemed Cybil still couldn't quite accept what had happened, as he was clutching his head and staggering around.

"O-one hit... A blunt attack... Not a slash... And in one hit...? Why was I...so happy over a single head...?"

"Ah, well, the Executioner is a special case, so don't sweat it too much."

"D-dammiiiiiit!! I'm gonna get strongeeer!!" Cybil yelled and ran straight off in tears.

"...Well, I could've seen that coming..." Unable to do anything as he watched the boy go, Jade scratched his cheek.

The kid was a frontline attacker, the same as the Executioner, so you really couldn't blame him. If an incredibly strong tank showed up and took out the opponent they'd been struggling against in a single hit, then maybe Jade would feel emotionally overwhelmed, too.

Incidentally, a few days later, Cybil announced that he was going to quit Silver Sword to go off training, so Silver Sword ultimately found themselves back at the drawing board over their longstanding issue of lacking a frontline attacker.

7

"I-it's so unusual for you to come to the guild headquarters, Alina. What's going on? Do you have a stomachache?" Jade asked with much trepidation.

They were in the guildmaster's office, sitting before the heavy desk in the back of the room. After the Executioner—aka Alina—had suddenly charged into the training area, they had swiftly tossed her in here. Once she'd finally cooled down, they asked her what was going on.

Alina, hood off, was still furious. Her eyes were glazed over with anger. "Don't give me that crap... You tell *me* what's going on, you stupid adventurer boss..."

"Stupid adventurer boss?!"

"Why! Are there! So many adventurers taking quests all of a sudden?! Explain yourself!" Alina demanded in fury.

Jade's shoulders hitched awkwardly. "Huh? There're already adventurers pouring in…?"

"*Already*? So you do know something?" Alina grabbed Jade by the lapels as she gave him an undeservedly murderous look. "The masses are out of control! They're flooding into Iffole Counter, and we've been struggling with them since morning…!"

Glen Garia calmly opened his mouth, grimacing behind his desk. "Calm down, li'l miss. I'll tell you."

Back in the day, Glen had been Silver Sword's frontline attacker, and his physique was no less impressive in the present; he emanated the dignity of a seasoned warrior. Wrinkles befitting a man of his age were carved in his sun-darkened skin, and now his rugged face had grown even more severe.

With a heavy sigh, Glen began to speak.

"The truth is—"

****

"A-a false rumor?!" Alina's pathetic cry rang out in the guildmaster's office.

"That's right. Word has suddenly started spreading among adventurers about a secret quest that will lead you to a relic that grants you a Dia skill. The adventurers rushing your office are probably in a rush to take up quests because they believe the rumor and want a Dia skill."

"Wh-why would a story like that be going around…? Where did it even come from?!"

"Since you found that secret quest recently, all everyone's talked about is hidden dungeons and special relics. Maybe the rumor started half as a joke…or it could be a prankster who wanted to cause confusion," Glen answered heavily.

Soberly, Jade added, "I've only just heard those rumors myself today... I never imagined that word would spread so fast."

"B-but still! This is strange! Who would believe a clearly fishy story about a relic that can get you a Dia ski..." Alina trailed off in the middle of her rant. She didn't even have to ask. Because a whole bunch of adventurers who had been convinced by the rumor had crammed into her workplace.

When Alina fell silent, Jade answered reluctantly. "...It may be difficult for you to understand, but if it really were possible to get a Dia skill, that would basically guarantee your success as an adventurer. The prospect would have us watering at the mouth."

"But...but! Skills are something you're born with, aren't they?!" Alina pressed Jade. Even after having it explained to her, she just couldn't accept everything at work had gone to hell over a single rumor. She would be far more easily convinced to hear that they had found over ten new dungeons at the same time, or some super-large dungeon was finally right about to be cleared after ten years— something like that.

But a story? She couldn't accept that her deluge of overtime had been deliberately manufactured.

"...Yeah. There's never been an example of someone acquiring a skill from an external source, so it really seems improbable, but... those doubts aside, a Dia skill is still attractive. Adventurers who aren't satisfied with the skills they've manifested, especially those without any to their name, would leap at the chance to get a Dia skill without hesitation. I bet there are some unscrupulous types who see this as an opportunity to make money, too. A lot of people who would do anything to acquire a Dia skill."

That did explain the abnormal enthusiasm. Now that Jade had gone into more detail about it, Alina finally understood why things were so strange at the receptionist counter.

It wasn't simply that a vast number of adventurers had surged into the office. Their eyes had all been goggling, and they'd been kicking one another down, not even caring how they looked as they scrambled to go first. They'd even abandoned all traces of basic reason and orderliness—just like a mob.

"..." Alina was unable to say anything more, so she closed her lips with a groan.

Unlike magic, skills couldn't be attained through book learning or training. The people who did get skills all received a different one at birth, and the harsh reality was that you would never be able to use a skill if you never manifested one. Consequently, skills had a far greater effect in combat than magic. In fact, your success in life might even be guaranteed if you manifested a particularly desirable skill.

Whether or not you developed a skill came down to luck, and even if you did get one, there was no guarantee it would be what you wanted. Skills weren't reliably useful, and they couldn't be developed through effort, yet that didn't change the fact they were a vital tool for adventuring. It was little wonder, then, that the adventurers who had to cope with these unfair circumstances had gone into a frenzy over the sweet temptation of a relic that could grant someone a Dia skill.

"...Hold on a minute. Then how do we make things settle down...?" With a gasp, Alina came to a terrifying realization. "Usually, things die down at the reception counter once someone takes care of the floor boss the adventurers are stuck on, but..."

"Well..." After pausing in hesitation, Jade looked away and continued speaking. "I guess it's until the rumor dies down..."

A heavy silence fell.

"...N-no way...," Alina stuttered. It sounded pathetic, even to her.

The strength in her legs gave out, and she crumpled to the expensive carpet. Her mind had gone blank, and she felt as though she would be blown away like sand if a gust of wind came by.

"But...the Cen...the Centennial Festival... is only a week away...

If this keeps up every day…and we go into the special bonus period…then…there won't be any time for the festival." Her voice gradually started to quiver before she bit her lip.

Until now, even when it had seemed like there was no end to Alina's overtime in sight, things had gone back to normal after the boss holding everything up was defeated. And in those cases, it didn't matter who killed the boss, adventurer or otherwise. Let's say a receptionist got fed up with overtime and decided to take care of the offending creature herself—that would still stop all the extra work.

But things were different this time. There was no boss for Alina to kill, no dungeon for her to finish. Her usual feats of strength would not work here. She would have to keep chugging along through this hellish period of overtime, all because of these rumors that showed no sign of dying down.

That meant she was guaranteed to have overtime during this year's Centennial Festival as well. Upon reaching this conclusion, Alina just about burst into tears.

"I-it'll be okay, Alina!" Seeing her unusually upset, Jade panicked. "At the end of the day, a story's just a story. Tomorrow, the guild will be announcing that the information about Dia skills is fake, and if the person circulating the rumor stops spreading it, then there won't be any more upro—"

"Are adventurers the kind of levelheaded people who will give up after a single warning…?"

"Urk!"

"They aren't, are they…? It seems like even more of them are ignoring guild warnings and trying to find secret quests lately, and the number of quests has been quietly increasing, too…"

"W-well…"

Even an organization as powerful as the guild had a hard time controlling adventurers, since they were freelancers. They were responsible for themselves and worked at their own discretion. They could ignore a direct warning from the guild at no personal risk. Just how many adventurers would believe the guild and stop taking quests after being told the rumors were fake?

"C'mon, it's not like all adventurers are like that. I think things will settle down a little..."

"...I get how things are, for now," Alina muttered, then got to her feet. "I'm going back...I have to finish up today's work... Complaining about these things won't decrease my overtime... The Centennial Festival won't wait for me..." She moved her body mechanically, grumbling all the while. "I'll do it... No matter what sort of hell awaits me... I won't give in...! I swear up and down that I'm going to enjoy the Centennial Festival...!"

8

"Alina seemed pretty tired..."

As Jade watched Alina zip back to Iffole Counter, Lululee Ashford came into the office to voice her concern.

Lululee was a cute girl with straight-cut bangs and a bob. She was shorter than the rod she carried, and to top it all off, she had a very babyish face. But despite her looks, she was a talented healer and a member of Silver Sword.

During the meeting with Alina, Lululee and Lowe had stood at the entrance to subtly drive people off. They couldn't afford to let a mysterious person dressed like the Executioner be seen openly speaking with the guildmaster in his office.

"Looks like that rumor has caused a lot of adventurers to go surging into the offices...," said Lowe Losblender with a shrug. He had come in along with Lululee. The young man was dressed in all-black equipment below the neck: black mage robes, a black rod, and black boots. His monochromatic outfit made his blazing red hair stand out all the more. "I really feel bad for Alina."

"Hmm, I'd like to help her with overtime, but it looks like lots of other receptionists are staying behind, too. I really can't go today," said Jade.

"Huh? How can you tell that, leader?" Lowe blinked with a puzzled expression.

Jade proudly stuck up his index finger and answered, "By her smell, of course."

""...Smell...?""

Lululee and Lowe asked in unison, both their faces twitching a little for some reason. They stared at him with scorn in their eyes.

"Alina smelled like the other receptionists' perfume. She never wears perfume or does anything fashion conscious like that, so... Huh, why are you glaring at me?"

"I know your eyes and nose are unusually keen, but I feel like you're using them the wrong way... Are you a dog, leader...?" said Lowe.

"I think you're on the road to getting sued, Jade," Lululee agreed.

"I haven't done anything bad!"

"It's about how it feels."

"..."

Why did he have to get laid into like this just from having smelled something and analyzed the scent? Jade tilted his head in dissatisfaction. But as he caught sight of Lululee's face, he recalled feeling like something had been off during their training session earlier.

"Oh yeah, Lululee. In that mock battle, I felt like you were hesitating more than usual before casting that heal—was something the matter?"

Jade hadn't meant anything by the question, but the reaction he got was a little unexpected.

"...Huh?" Lululee widened her eyes, like she was startled. "I-I've never fought in a party with a greatsword wielder, so that's why."

"...I see."

Lululee's face was a little pale, and she answered rather quickly, as if trying to hide that she was upset. It seemed like she wasn't telling him something—that's what Jade figured at least. Her suddenly pulling out a poor lie must have meant she didn't want to talk about it, so Jade didn't press her any further.

"Lulu, we got done faster than we planned, so let's go out to eat for once! Whoever loses rock-paper-scissors pays!" Lowe said cheerfully, wrapping an arm around Lululee's shoulders. She hit him with her rod.

9

The next day...

"Six more days until the Centennial Festival...! That's less than a week...!" Alina checked the wall calendar in the offices of Iffole Counter.

Surrounded by absurdly large piles of documents yet again that day, Alina was getting through her work at a feverish pace.

Office hours were already over, and the darkness of night had taken hold outside. It had been a long time since she'd started overtime, but the mountain of remaining work was still so high that she couldn't bring herself to take a break yet.

"Urk, I'm going to call it a day soon..." With a heavy, dejected sigh, Laila lay her face down on her desk, out of energy.

"I can't believe this was caused by a rumor...and now of all times, too. It's too much... Wahhhh."

"But there is less work here than yesterday. I wonder if those dumbasses' heads cooled a bit from getting told off by the guild."

"Please don't say that like you're ready to murder someone..."

Ignoring Laila's complaints, Alina shifted her gaze to the brochure that was placed on the corner of her desk like a charm for protection. It was the guidebook for the Centennial Festival. A few months back, she'd written all there was to know about the event in it, so she could enjoy this year's festival to the fullest.

It would not be exaggerating to say that the guidebook was the only thing keeping Alina going.

"You're still going to keep at it, Alina?"

"Of course. It's not done yet," she answered immediately.

"…" Laila mumbled under her breath as if in protest. After a few seconds of that, she finally said to Alina, "Hey, why don't you slow down on the forms a bit?"

"Huh?" The unexpected proposal made Alina lift her head, where her eyes met with Laila's.

Laila looked a little uneasy. "You're the fastest at handling the forms…so you're processing double the amount."

"…Well, maybe that's true…"

In order to handle the line at her reception window when things were crowded, Alina would skip everything that wasn't immediately necessary so she could process quest forms as fast as possible. The other receptionists, on the other hand, would deliberately take a little time filling out their forms to reduce the total number they would be responsible for. The adventurers who got sick of waiting would come back another day or wander to another reception window.

Laila was slow at the job out of pure inexperience, which nevertheless ended up limiting the amount of work on her plate.

She must have been rather sharp if she'd learned how to pull off one of adulthood's secret techniques—deliberately slacking to a degree that's not unacceptable but not quite kosher either—in only her first year of employment.

"Just holding back a bit and listening for a while to the adventurers who brag about themselves will reduce the number of quests you handle by quite a bit. That's what all the older receptionists do, you know? That's why none of them have that much overtime! It's unfair for you to shoulder all the burden. You already have to do the quest totaling at the end of day... At least slow down a bit until the end of the Centennial Festival."

"Listen, even if we all drag our feet, that won't decrease the number of adventurers who come to the office. In the end, someone's gotta do it."

"That's true...but it doesn't have to be you...! Someone else will get to it eventually!"

"I do agree with you..." Alina gave Laila a weary nod before she flicked her eyes away and added quietly, "But I don't like to do petty things like that."

"That's just playing into the boss's hands, Alina...!"

10

Late that night, Jade was sitting on a sofa in an empty room.

Also there were the other members of Silver Sword, Lowe and Lululee, as well as Guildmaster Glen and Fili, his private secretary. They were all facing one another around a low table.

Since there was a strong possibility that the story about the relic could lead to the resurrection of a dark god, they were holding a secret emergency meeting.

In the heavy silence, Jade kicked things off. "A rumor, huh...?" he muttered. "How strange. Why is it going around now, of all times?"

It was true that adventurers did frequently swap information in offices and taverns, and through their interactions in dungeons. This caused information to circulate quickly—and occasionally, false information would spread in this manner as well.

"It just seems to me like the story has exploded since everyone learned the bit about getting a Dia skill... Does something about this feel off to you?" asked Lululee.

"This is exactly like the time with Rufus," Jade pointed out, and everyone present gulped.

One month ago, an adventurer named Rufus had killed his own allies to revive a dark god. He'd resented Silver Sword and plotted to kill them all using that dark god, but ultimately lost his life to the very being he'd awakened.

"Rufus was confident about there being a relic that can give you a Dia skill in a hidden dungeon. This is the same kind of rumor. It's difficult to imagine that's a coincidence." Lowe picked up on what Jade was trying to say. "So there's someone who incited Rufus, and they're deliberately spreading around this story, too...?"

"It's possible. Someone who knew about the dark god could have told Rufus about him to eliminate Silver Sword, then sent him to the White Tower. And now this same person is spreading a rumor about a relic that can grant Dia skills to get low-level adventurers riled up and make them find hidden dungeons."

"..." Lowe fell silent listening to Jade's inferences. His face was white with fear; he must have been imagining what someone who knew of the dark gods could be after. "...You mean they're using adventurers to try to revive the dark gods...?"

"That's what I'm forced to assume." Jade wanted to deny it, if possible, but he sighed and nodded.

The dark gods who slumbered in hidden dungeons could come back to life by devouring human souls. To be blunt, anyone could revive one, so long as they had a life to offer.

"What the hell are they thinking? What an awful human being...," Lowe muttered bitterly with a grimace. No surprise there. The dark god that Jade's party Silver Sword had fought a month ago had been an incredibly powerful foe, the likes of which they'd never experienced before.

No—the dark gods went beyond merely "powerful foes."

They could use multiple Dia skills—the highest category of skill—and were highly resistant to attack. Using these qualities, they'd wiped out the ancients in a single night. It was unlikely that modern humans would ever be able to match up with them in terms of technology or power. The dark gods were practically a force of nature.

"You have a point, Jade." Glen, who had been patiently listening until now, finally spoke up. "We can't just chalk the many commonalities between this rumor and what Rufus did up to coincidence. Someone is certainly pulling the strings behind the scenes. If not for the li'l miss... I shudder to think what would have happened if that dark god left the White Tower and made it into town."

Though Glen didn't say anything more, everyone could easily imagine that gruesome future.

Long ago, the ancients who dwelled on the continent of Helcacia had possessed advanced technologies and powerful abilities called Dia skills. But one night, they vanished from the face of the earth, leaving ruins in their wake. The commonly accepted theory was that the ancients' greedy desires for research had enraged the gods into destroying them—but that wasn't quite what had happened.

In truth, the ancients had fashioned relics known as "dark gods," who possessed incredible bodies and powers. Ironically, it was these very beings that destroyed the ancients' legacy in a single night.

If such dangerous gods were unleashed from the secret dungeons, humanity would unquestionably meet the same fates as the ancients. Jade's gut turned ice cold as he thought of this again. There were still many more of those dangerous entities slumbering somewhere on this continent.

"If the same thing happened again and a dark god revived...," Jade said.

Lowe and the others all gulped. Sudden silence fell upon them, and that suffocating quiet continued for a few seconds—

"Hey, um."

*   *   *

Suddenly, a low voice cut in.

Everyone raised their heads, turning their eyes to the person who'd spoken.

The cold lights of the room lit mountains of quest forms. The shelves were packed with stored documents, and the desks were neatly arranged. From one of these desks, which had a mountain of forms both atop and around it somehow, emanated a depressing aura—someone glared daggers at them.

It was Alina, having a glorious day of overtime.

"Never mind about the dark god... Why are all you guys gathered here...? I'm in the middle of overtime right now..."

Yes, the place where Jade and company had gathered was the office of Iffole Counter. They were using the desk and sofa for guests to hold their emergency meeting.

"I do feel bad, but cut us some slack this time, li'l miss—oh, this is for you."

Breaking the heavy air with a guffaw, Guildmaster Glen of the Adventurers Guild, not fundamentally the type of person who should be in a modest place like this, scratched his head. His private secretary Fili, who stood at his side, quietly held out a basket of snacks for Alina.

"We can't just go talking about you or things related to the dark gods and whatnot at guild headquarters. You never know who might be listening in. You don't want outsiders hearing about this either, right?"

"But there's got to be some other place to talk! Can you not whisper about such depressing stuff right where I'm trying to work overtime?!"

"Come on, Alina. Once this meeting is over, we'll help you with your extra work."

"So you say, but you're trying to get me dragged into this one too, aren't you?!"

"Urk!"

"I'm not falling for that…! Just so you know, I'll have nothing to do with those dark gods or whatever! Handling them is your job!"

"Y-you're completely right…" Having no room for counterargument, Glen was left groaning.

Beside him, Jade lowered his voice in concern. "More importantly, are you eating properly, Alina…? Your cheeks look pretty gaunt… They say that when you lose weight, it comes from your chest, so you should make sure to ea—"

"What was that?!" Alina silenced Jade with a murderous glare.

Lululee cut in with concern, "Alina, I told you that it's bad for you to drink too many potions…! When you're tired, you should drink something with a relaxing effect, like herbal tea…"

"A fancy drink like that isn't going to offset how exhausted I am from overwork…"

"Eeep!"

"I'm a pretty decent cook. I'll make you something nutritious later, Alina."

"I don't care about nutrition! The one thing I want is the Centennial Festival!" Eyebrows furrowing even further, Alina snapped her feather pen in her fist. "Just so you know, this is an emergency situation for me, too…!"

Ignoring Lululee's advice, Alina tossed back a potion, friend to everyone who burned the midnight oil, and bared her teeth in an intimidating glare. "This isn't just overtime…! My…my chance to attend the Centennial Festival is hanging on by a—" Before she could finish her sentence, Alina suddenly swallowed her words, as if she'd realized something. A moment later, her eyes suddenly sparkled as she turned to Glen. "I know! If you stop time with your skill, Guildmaster, then couldn't I finish up my remaining work and make it home on schedule?!"

Sigurth Chronos was Glen's skill for stopping time. It was a very rare skill, and back when he'd been in the field, it had garnered him a reputation as the strongest adventurer of all.

But Glen sadly rejected Alina's idea. "Sorry, but that's impossible, li'l miss. Even if my skill can stop time, it doesn't allow you to intervene in events. Time will never move for anyone but me—and you, I guess, since you're the exception—so if you try to do your office work while *Sigurth Chronos* is active, your feather pen won't move, and neither will anything else."

"...No way..."

Upon further reflection, there was no way such a highly convenient skill would exist, but Alina was willing to grasp at straws at this point.

Her gaze fell despondently, and she turned to a booklet, nearly buried beneath piles of documents, on a section of her desk. It was a festival guidebook, the one handed out to tourists every year as the Centennial Festival drew near.

Jade peered at the worn-out guidebook cover and saw that Alina had jotted down every bit of information she'd gathered about the Centennial Festival on it. If the cover alone was already overflowing with details, he figured there was much more on the inside. Alina had been abnormally fixated on the event the day before, going on about the Centennial Festival this, the Centennial Festival that; she was looking forward to it with a highly unusual degree of enthusiasm.

"Maybe...I won't be able to go to the Centennial Festival this year after all... Wah... Wahh..."

"Alina..."

Jade was at a loss for words as he watched Alina sob pitifully, drowning in overtime. Amid this atmosphere fit for a graveyard, he laid a gentle hand on Alina's small, trembling shoulder. "It's too early to give up yet, Alina."

"Huh?" She raised her head with a start.

Jade flashed her a reliable smile and pointed at himself with his thumb. "Aren't you forgetting something? Like that you have a savio—"

"I forgot," Alina answered instantly, not letting him finish.

"Uh, you're clearly thinking of it now!" Jade grew flustered. "If I put in some serious effort to help you with your extra work, then we can finish two or three times the amount in the same number of hours! Mark my words, I'll take you to the Centennial Festival!"

"This is you we're talking about, so I know you're gonna add in some weird condition full of ulterior motives!"

"Urk!"

Alina really was sharp. She was 100 percent right.

"Oh, I was just thinking that, in exchange for helping you with your overtime, I'd like to go on a date with you at the Centennial Festival."

"Who would accept a condition like that?!"

"Then just two days…no, one day! One day is fine! I'll take one day, so let's go on a date!"

"I would genuinely rather die!"

"Y-you're that against it…?!" After such a thorough rejection, now it was Jade's turn to cry.

"It seems like you've got the wrong idea here. When I want to enjoy something from the bottom of my heart, I want to experience it by myself. I don't want to worry about a companion and be forced to bow to their whims! I'm the type who likes to go shopping and do stuff alone, too!"

If she was going to be like that, Jade wouldn't even have a razor's width of room to squeeze in. But he refused to be discouraged, gritting his teeth as he drew closer to her. "Ngh…but Alina! You've never been to the festival before, so you might not know this, but there are lots of guys trying to pick up girls there! A cute lady walking on her own is basically asking to get hit on! They call them 'easy pickings'! But you won't have to worry about that if I'm with you."

"Just so you know, you're exactly as annoying as guys like that."

"Then it's better to be with a nuisance who you at least know, right?"

"Why would you think that?!"

"So then a date with m—"

"No! Why do I have to let some pushy guys keep me from doing what I want?"

"But the way things are going right now, you attending the Centennial Festival isn't even a guarantee," Jade pointed out.

"Ngh!" Alina was choked silent. Then she dropped her head and started to mutter, "But... No, it's true... I really can't deal with all of this alone..."

Pressing her lips into a line, she glared at the documents. "Small sacrifices...may be required... The Centennial Festival is three days in total... If I resign myself to spending just one day with this lug, then I can enjoy the other two days... Even if I feel so awful I could puke for one day, I can cancel that out with the other two days..."

"Sometimes, you say what you're thinking aloud, Alina... I know that's deliberate..."

"Fine." Finally giving in, Alina agreed to Jade's terms with much annoyance.

"R-really?!"

"But in exchange! I'm *absolutely* going to the Centennial Festival...! We're going to beat the hell out of this overtime!"

"Leave it to me! Let's do our best, Alina."

"...Ahh, you two." Seeing that their discussion had finally concluded, Glen took the opportunity to awkwardly raise his voice. "Your couple's comedy routine is nice and all, but can we get back to the subject at hand— *Bff*?!"

Alina instantly hurled her fist into Glen's face, sending the large man tumbling over, sofa and all.

Fili, who had lurking by his side like a shadow, blanched and dashed over to him. "G-Guildmaster?!"

"Hey... I'm on edge here, from overtime... Any more of that

kind of careless, old-fashioned dad kind of teasing, and I'll break your two front teeth…"

"S-sorry…"

Tottering as he returned the sofa to its original position, Glen cleared his throat, and as he was trying to get back to the subject at hand…

There came a thudding sound, and the mountain of mixed documents that had been piled up on a nearby shelf all came crashing down.

This drew a bewildered "Huh?" from Jade as the fall triggered a chain reaction right in front of him. Nearby paper mountains collapsed one after another, burying the floor in masses of forms in the blink of an eye.

Jade's jaw dropped. "No way…are these all…unprocessed documents…?!"

"…That's right…," Alina replied as she staggered over to clean up the mountains of papers. Jade had thought for sure that the ones piled on Alina's desk were all of them, but apparently, he had been naive. Unable to stand by and do nothing, Lululee and Lowe went over to pitch in as Alina slowly crumpled the document in her hand.

"I've had enough…I've had enough…!" Tears beading in her jade-green eyes, she glared at Glen a beat later. "Hey… The other day, you said someone was deliberately circulating the rumor about the relic, right…?!"

"Y-yeah…that's highly prob—"

Alina didn't even let him finish, tossing away the document in her hand to grab Glen by his lapels. "Tell whoever is spreading that story that I'm going to kill them myself…!"

The force of Alina's stare alone was enough to kill a man ten times over, and it even made a seasoned adventurer like Glen shake in his boots.

"W-well, we've somewhat narrowed down the source of the story, but we still don't know who it is for certain yet… And even if you beat up whoever is spreading the rumor, it's not like that will take care of your overtime…"

"Tell me." With her face twisted in resentment and rage, Alina bared her teeth as she leaned toward Glen. "They're still shamelessly spreading around that story, aren't they…? And they're continuing to convince adventurers that it's true, correct…? I can't leave them alive for another minute, another second. Isn't that right?!"

"…W-well, that is indeed inexcusable. Though I want to get some information out of this rumormonger, so I'd like you to leave them alive."

"This year's Centennial Festival…is my reason for living!! The freedom and dignity of a humble receptionist and laborer hangs on this event!! And they have the nerve to…try and crush that with some stupid rumor!! Well, I won't let them! I'll kill them with my own two hands!!"

Alina's howl of rage echoed through the late-night office. Her wild wrath, with not even a word of consolation following, left the office frozen.

11

It was five days until the Centennial Festival.

Alina was walking through the depths of a thick forest.

It was a C-class dungeon called the Forest of Eternity. These woods were unique.

Typically, only buildings constructed by the ancients were referred to as "dungeons," but the Forest of Eternity was a seemingly ordinary forest. Yet it was still considered a dungeon.

That was because it was full of the ether that could only be found in the ruins of the ancients, which meant that many monsters, who were attracted to the ether, had taken up residence there.

That being said, the creatures in the Forest of Eternity were not that strong, and the dungeon had only a single level. Each floor of a dungeon typically had an area where the ether was strongest—otherwise known as a boss room—but the sprawling Forest of Eternity lacked one. Perhaps the increased airflow outdoors allowed the ether to distribute evenly across the area.

The woods weren't too far from Iffole, so you could go back to town without even using the crystal gate. For that reason, the Forest of Eternity was valued by beginner adventurers as a training ground.

"Finding this person must be a big deal if you're using your precious time off to do it…," Jade muttered as he walked beside Alina along a pathless way between the trees.

"I'm going to destroy that rumormonger. It'll be okay. I've told Laila she can go it alone."

"*You traitor, Alina!!*" Laila had moaned, her face a mess of snot and tears. But you had to lose a Laila to win this one—rather, lose a battle to win the war. Otherwise, this catastrophe would never come to an end. Some sacrifices were inevitable.

"Just so you know," Jade said, "if the one who's spreading this rumor is the same person who instigated Rufus, then I want to question them. Please don't kill them by accident."

"I'll do my best."

"…"

"But wait, is the person spreading the stories really out here…? Not at a tavern or something?" Alina closely examined the forest around her once more.

They were surrounded by towering trees with tangled foliage formed into a natural roof that blocked out the light of the sun. Even though it was the middle of the day, the forest was dim and the air was cool, with roots shooting up from the ground that made it hard to navigate.

"A lot of adventurers come here. It's not a bad place to disseminate information. And besides, the adventurers who gather at taverns are generally drunk, so you can't have a decent conversation with them."

"...I see. That aside..." Though she was convinced by Jade's explanation, Alina pinched the edge of the robe she was wearing and made a face. "Just what is up with this costume?"

Right now, Alina was *not* clad in the cloak she normally wore as the Executioner. She was covered in the robe of a white mage, the hood obscuring her face, and carrying an unfamiliar magic rod.

Alina wasn't the only one in an unusual getup. Jade had donned a black mage's robe and was holding a long rod, Lowe was in light armor and had a longsword at his waist, while Lululee had a tank's greatshield on her back. The healer looked less like she was carrying a shield and more like the shield was carrying her.

"...Take a look at Lululee... The shield is so much bigger than her body that she looks like a shield with legs from behind...," remarked Alina.

"Pffft, heh-heh, I've honestly been thinking the exact same thing. A shield wiggling around through the forest. It's hilarious," added Lowe.

"Lowe...! You'll pay for this...!" Lululee ground her teeth in frustration on the other side of the shield.

"Uh, I think having Alina in charge of healing is a lot more alarming, though...," said Jade.

"What are you trying to say here?" Alina glared at him.

Jade hurriedly started to explain the changes of outfits. "A-according to the stories the information team has gathered, the rumors are targeted at upstart adventurers. It's more convenient if they don't recognize that we're Silver Sword. These aren't costumes, they're disguises."

"Man, this equipment kind of takes me back." Lowe smiled, looking down at the cheap light armor for his disguise as a beginner adventurer. Just like all their equipment, it was the kind you could get on the cheap at the market—commonly circulated

weapons that you could find anywhere. "I'm getting flashbacks to when I was a beginner. In those days, even this kinda equipment made me happy. It felt like, *Yeah, I'm an adventurer!* Right, shield-monster?"

"Mgggg…!" Though Lululee was gritting her teeth again, Alina figured she didn't have a comeback, as she turned away with a *hmph*. The shield was in the way, so Alina couldn't see for sure.

"A beginner…" Suddenly she heard Lululee mumble from behind the shield. "…Yeah."

She must have been tired, as her voice sounded a little listless.

12

"Here it is," said Jade.

Hearing that, Alina came to a stop. Following Jade's directions, they had arrived at a lush clearing that contained a small body of water.

"A lake…?" she wondered.

It was a strange lake with a large boulder smack in the middle, as if it had fallen from the sky. The mossy green boulder had a solemn air about it, while the surface of the water, sparkling under the midday sun, looked anything but dungeon-like.

"Mossy Rock Lake," Jade explained. "It's a well-known rest spot among adventurers. The ether is thinner here, so it doesn't see many monsters."

Indeed, the footpath here was well-worn, and it looked like a few logs and stumps had been used as seating—signs that many adventurers used this place to rest.

"We'll take a little break here," he said.

"Huh…?"

Ignoring Alina's questioning, Jade slowly set down his weapon and started to relax, leaving himself unguarded like an inexperienced adventurer.

"Well, if our leader says so, then I guess we're resting," said Lowe.

Shrugging in resignation, Lowe and Lululee both put down their weapons and sat down. Lululee gave a big stretch, happy to be rid of the heavy shield. Alina also sat down eagerly.

"M-my shoulders are so stiff..." Lululee groaned.

"I chose a lighter one, though... This is why I said you should pick a round shield that you can equip on one arm," said Jade.

"But I can't hide my face with that." Lululee's face twisted in regret. "When I first picked it up, I thought it would work...!"

"Well, yeah, carrying it for a moment and carrying it for a long time are two different things."

"When it gets too much for me, I'll switch with Alina..."

"Hey!"

"By the way, Alina." His expression suddenly meek, Jade stared at Alina.

"What?"

"This lake is pretty deep, and the water is clear. I hear it feels nice to swim in. Most of the beginner adventurers around here will play a game where they race to touch the mossy rock and back."

"Uh-huh."

"Wanna brighten the mood with a swim?" Jade invited her in the most direct way possible, putting on a very cool and serious look. Pleased with himself, he continued, "Of course, I've already got a bathing suit for you t— *Gerf*!"

Alina grabbed Jade by the back of his head and wordlessly shoved him into the lake. "Go drown to death, you deviant silver scum."

"Brgle grgle!"

Watching from afar as Jade flailed under the water and Alina coldly looked down on him, Lowe and Lululee, being entirely used to such scenes, leisurely gulped down their bottled drinks and sighed.

"That one was Jade's fault," remarked Lululee.

"Yeah, I agree," added Lowe.

"Hey, you guys look like you're enjoying yourselves," came a gentle male voice all of a sudden as a party appeared at the banks of the lake.

It was a group of four men. The oldest of them, a middle-aged healer who looked like the leader, asked them amicably, "Are you guys resting here, too?"

"Yes, we're still beginners. We're training in the Forest of Eternity," Jade smoothly lied in a slightly higher-pitched voice than usual. He'd gotten out of Alina's clutches at some point.

"Ohh, you've got spirit. Then how about we join you for a while to rest? My name is Heitz, by the way. Nice to meet you."

No sooner had he plopped down on the ground than he began some carefree chitchat.

13

"Say, do you kids know about secret quests?" Heitz suddenly brought up, after they had been talking for a while.

"Secret quests?" Jade, who had been chatting with him, tilted his head and pretended he didn't know.

"Yes. I suppose you haven't heard yet, since you're beginners. There's a hidden dungeon on this continent that nobody knows about… People have been saying that for ages. Apparently, it'll show up if you take a secret quest."

"Is there something valuable there?"

"…Of course. The dungeon holds a special relic. I suppose the most straightforward way to put it would be to say…it's a relic that can manifest a Dia skill."

"A Dia skill?!"

"Heh-heh. It sounds like a dream, doesn't it? The most powerful class of skills, now lost to time... If you could get your hands on one of those, then you wouldn't have to practice in a place like this. You could become powerful in an instant."

"Yeah...!" Jade said, sounding pure and eager, just like a newbie—before his expression suddenly darkened, and his voice went low. "But is that true?"

Heitz suddenly stiffened, then backed away upon seeing Jade's composure change. Jade kept his eyes locked on Heitz as he pulled off the hood that had been hanging over his face.

"Jade Scrade from Silver Sword?!"

Heitz blanched, realizing that he was the one who'd been had. His friends also panicked and rose to their feet, but Alina and the others had already surrounded them, eliminating their avenues of escape.

"Ngh...!"

"You lay in wait at this break spot, and whenever a party shows up, you pretend like you just stumbled upon them and strike up a conversation... So that's how you've been spreading those rumors," said Jade.

"Silver Sword... Did the guild put you up to this...? They're quick on the uptake."

"Are you the one who instigated Rufus, too?"

"Rufus...? I don't know him. We just heard about Dia skills from a man in black."

"A man in black...?" With a start, Jade drew the rod from his belt, blocking the sword of a man who'd tried to slash at him.

He was a tank with an eye patch over his left eye and a greatshield on his back. The man gave a low, bold chuckle. "You even went to the effort of putting on those goofy disguises. Who would've thought that Silver Sword would come out here over just some rumor. Sounds like you guys really have a lot of time on your—"

And then the man vanished, his remark cut off.

No, he'd been slammed sideways by something terrifying. A moment later, the man skidded backward with a *kssssssh*, gouging a groove into the earth as he went.

"""" """"
...

That attack was so merciless, it struck both enemy and ally dumb. Everyone turned their gazes to a single point...to the person who had smacked the tank away without so much as a good-bye, refusing to listen to his insulting remark.

It was Alina, swaying in anger, her war hammer in hand.

"So you've finally shown yourself, you filthy rumormonger...," Alina muttered in a low voice, an incredibly murderous aura oozing out from underneath the healing robes of a white mage. "Die."

"Th-that skill! And that war hammer! ...Is that the Executioner?!" Heitz widened his eyes when he saw her weapon. "So the things people said about you joining Silver Sword were true...?!" He glanced at his allies behind him like he was going to try something, then thrust his arm out.

Alina ignored this and readied her war hammer. That was when it happened.

"P-please wait!" Lululee cried out. "Aiden...is that you, Aiden?!" She was looking at the tank who had been slammed aside. The desperate tone of her voice stayed Alina's hands for a moment.

Heitz took advantage of that opening to yell, "Skill Activate: *Sigurth Mover*!" The red light of his skill surged out over the banks of the lake. Alina readied herself for an attack, but the red light of the Sigurth skill that flowed from Heitz's hands was directed not at his enemies but at his own party. The glow immediately enveloped Heitz and the two men behind him—and then, in an instant, they were gone.

"They disappeared...?!"

"So it was a teleportation skill...!" Jade had surmised this from its similarities to the warping abilities of the crystal gate. Next, his eyes fell on the tank. Left behind by his allies, the man was battered, his cloak torn apart and his body exposed by the impact of the blow he'd taken.

He had no right arm. That, along with his bandaged eye, put him at a serious disadvantage as a heavyweight greatshield bearer. No— it was beyond a disadvantage. Without an arm, you couldn't even tank in the first place, since you wouldn't be able to carry a sword and shield at the same time.

"Do you know this guy, Lululee?" Jade asked with a stern expression.

Lululee remained silent, unable to reply. But after examining the man for a few moments, she nodded clearly. "That…arm and eye… It can't be anyone else. He's…my old…"

"Heh…heh-heh!" A low laugh slipped from the man Lululee had called Aiden, cutting her off. He didn't seem bothered that his allies had left him behind and gave a shrug.

"My, oh my. Well if it isn't Ms. Healer."

"…So it really is you, Aiden…" Lululee gripped her rod tight. Her expression was grim and clouded with guilt.

"Why…? Why would you do something like this…? What are you spreading misinformation for?!"

"Misinformation? Nah. Dia skills are real," Aiden muttered darkly. "And what gives you the right to lecture me, huh? Lulu the murderer!"

For a moment, silence fell on the carefree banks of the lake.

"…Murderer?" Jade murmured, brow furrowing. He looked to Lululee automatically—but even being spoken to so cruelly, Lululee just hung her head silently, making no effort to deny Aiden's accusations.

"If you keep that little squirt with you as a healer, you're gonna bite the dust eventually. She's a murderer, and she's got no problem with abandoning her allies! *Gya-ha-ha-ha—hrk?!*"

Aiden cackled loudly, reveling in his monologue, only to be

blasted sideways abruptly, smacked in the cheek with a war hammer by someone who didn't have time for his shit.

"*Hegh!* Gah!"

He bounced along the ground multiple times as he rolled, plunging into the shallow water of the lake with a splash when he finally came to a stop. Aiden staggered to his feet, at a loss about what happened. Once he saw Alina coming a step ahead of the confused members of Silver Sword, war hammer in hand, however, he seemed to basically get it.

"Wh-what the hell? I was talking...!"

"Right now, it doesn't matter whether Lululee is a murderer or not, you third-rate loser..."

"Th-third rate? H-hey, it does matter!"

"I've suffered so much...because of the rumor you were thoughtlessly spreading around! A single story can emotionally devastate the laborers fighting on the front lines at work and ruin the event they've been looking forward to for so long... Do you understand the pain you've inflicted on receptionists...?"

"Huh?"

Eyes flashing, Alina readied her war hammer without giving Aiden a chance to argue. The fact that she wasn't wearing her usual Executioner's cloak but the outfit of a white mage—a healer—made her murderous aura come off as all the more violent.

"I let the other three vermin go... But I promised...that I'd kill whoever spread that rumor!!"

"Hey, hey, hey, hey, wait! I'm right about to tell you about that killer healer's past—"

"Shut up!! I can ask Lululee herself about that drawn-out sob story later!! Dieeeeeeeee!!"

"W-waaaaaaaugh!"

Aiden's shriek rang out through the afternoon forest. An instant later, the trees of the woods shuddered, and every bird that had been resting their wings flew into the air.

14

It was four days until the Centennial Festival.

The day before, they had succeeded in capturing one of the culprits who had been spreading rumors in the Forest of Eternity, but Alina's expression was dark. In the end, they hadn't managed to pin down the location of the three who had escaped.

However, Glen figured that since their identities had been exposed, they couldn't keep spreading stories. The guild's information team traced the whereabouts of Heitz and his friends, publicizing their names and faces and putting up wanted posters. That should be enough to stop the rumors for the time being.

The moment Alina stepped into Iffole Counter, Laila leaped on her and burst into tears. "Alina, where did you go yesterdaaaaaaaay?! It was so…it was so tough…! Mostly for me…! You always help me out, but you weren't there…!"

"I suddenly contracted a mysterious illness."

"Your voice sounded pretty lively, though?!"

"When your coworker is taking time off due to a 'weird stomachache' or a 'headache they've had all morning' or other dubious reasons…you should just use your head and accept that they're not feeling well… Got it?"

"What the heck is this newfangled common sense?!"

"All right! Time to work hard today… Since it's almost time for the Centennial Festival!"

****

Wave after wave of customers crashed against her reception window again that day, until Iffole Counter finally closed…

Almost everyone else had left, but Alina was staring wearily at a mountain of paperwork in the office.

"We caught the rumormonger…but I should've known that

things would take a while to go back to normal..." A deep sigh escaped her lips.

"That reminds me, they said they caught one of the people who was spreading the misinformation in today's paper...," Laila muttered idly. She was sprawled out on the visitor sofa, exhausted from that afternoon's work.

"That story was spreading like mad, so like Alina said, it's not going to die down right away...," said Jade quietly, putting a finger to his chin as he sat down at the desk next to Alina.

"By the way, um..." Laila, getting up from the sofa, suddenly grew serious as she tilted her head at Jade, who was sitting at that desk like he belonged there. "Um...that's my seat, Master Jade..." After saying that, Laila widened her eyes, as if the bizarreness of the sight was just hitting her. She forgot her exhaustion and began to tremble. "But wait...hold on a minute...! Why is the leader of Silver Sword and the strongest tank in the guild sitting at my desk like it's nothing and helping with Alina's overtime work?! What's happening?! Seriously, what is going on here?!"

"Well, it's exactly what it looks like."

"Just what it looks like," Alina replied at the same time as Jade, continuing to plug away at her forms nonchalantly. "I've got his help through a bit of a connection. It's okay, this lug can handle office work. More importantly, Laila, don't just wipe out there; come finish the rest of today's work. I can't spare even a single second today... I don't have the time to waste on this junk!"

"No...no, no, no, I can't! With Master Jade here and you calling him a 'lug' and 'junk,' it's more unreasonable to ask me to question nothing and just focus on the overtime..."

"Alina's promised me that if I help her with her overtime, she'll go on a date with me for a whole day of the Centennial Festival," Jade interjected from the side, offering way more information than necessary.

"Wh-what?!" Laila widened her eyes further in confusion. But then a few seconds later, her expression took a turn, and her eyes flashed. "Oh my…! I see…I see! If that's what's going on, then I'll be the cheerleader for your love, Master Jade!" Laila stood on the sofa and thrust a fist into the air. Her earlier exhaustion gone, she yelled, "I'm so happy…! Alina is so pretty, but her romantic life is six feet under! Like, there's no sign of men in her life—she doesn't dress up, and she doesn't try to flirt! Whenever a guy asks her out, she rejects him with this blank stare, and she looks at the adventurers who come to her window like they're less than insects! People even say they have absolutely no idea what she does on her days off, and um… It's kind of, like, this is very difficult to say to her face, but she does nothing but work and then withers up every day, respectfully speaking… So I've been thinking that she needs a little bit of richness in her life!"

"You're making fun of me, aren't you?"

"This is a form of love! I'm saying this out of concern for you! Master Jade, please. Alina has been saying that she's going to go to the Centennial Festival, an event crawling with couples, on her own! You *have* to stop her!"

"All right, leave it to me, Laila. By the way, I have something of a question here: Did you just say she was asked out? Does Alina get a lot of that?"

"Ahh, I sure envy how she's captured your affection… If you two get married, that means Alina will be moving up in the world! She can quit her job as a receptionist and live a life of leisure with her doting, handsome husband…"

"Why do I have to get married to this idiot? Can you not joke about that?"

"Huh?" Laila blinked her big eyes. "Whaaaat?! Is refusal even an option? Jade Scrade is a successful adventurer, you know! At the age of thirteen, he was already on the millionaire list, which features those adventurers who have earned the most reward sums for their

ages. People say that he's saved enough for a lifetime of leisure…!
And on top of that, he's tall, manly, handsome, and strong—"

"Yeah, yeah, he's amazing or whatever."

"And that greatshield that you're using right now as a stand to dry
the ink on your papers is worth years of income, you know!" Laila
pointed aggressively at Jade's shield. They'd wound up using it as a
document stand, since there was nowhere else to put all the excess
forms.

Now that Laila mentioned it, it was true Jade's greatshield had
been completely destroyed in the fight against Silha, so he must have
bought a new one. Relic arma were some of the rarest and costliest
relics out there, and in the worst case, they could command sums that
were more than the price of a house. His financial situation must
have been impressive indeed if he'd gotten a replacement so quickly.

But Alina rejected Laila's simplistic, low-class ideas. "You shut
up. In this world…there is such a thing as happiness that money
can't buy…"

"Hyeep!" Intimidated by Alina's glare, Laila let out a little shriek.

"A drink alone after work! Staying up late before a weekend! The
bliss of being able to have sweets all to yourself…!"

"That's so…so trivial…"

"But above all else…! That freedom comes *because* you earned
that money with your own sweat and blood, instead of getting it
from someone else! You can waste it! You can buy stupid things
without worrying about it! I would never be so simpleminded as to
rely on someone else's earnings!"

"…Master Jade, what is it that you like about Alina?"

"I actually rather enjoy how stubborn she is and how it seems like
she's had a bad lot in life," Jade replied nonchalantly. Laila couldn't
say a word.

"…Anyway, you're quite amazing at office work, you know that?"
Laila's eyes went wide as she gazed meekly at the documents Jade

had just processed, like she'd only noticed now. "You've been double-checking them for a while, but there isn't a single error…!"

Alina thrust out her bottom lip in a pout at Laila's shock. Yes, Jade was very good at processing documents. No—he was first-rate. And that wasn't the only thing he was amazing at.

"Oh, Alina, about that entry error I was mentioning before—" Jade brought over a quest form that an adventurer had filled out incorrectly, which one of the receptionists had accepted without noticing.

Normally, errors of that kind would be caught at the reception window, and the applicant would fill out a new form on the spot. If that didn't happen, those mistakes would be a real hassle to correct when you discovered them after the fact. At best, you would have to contact the person who'd filled it out at a later date, doubling your work. But if the mistake went undiscovered for a while, you would need the authority of the counter chief and even a stamp from an authority at the guild to resolve things. And if the staff in charge of rewards in the other department got wind of the mistake, then forget about it. You'd have to waste a ton of time writing reports and explaining things, all over a measly sheet of paper.

"I did some digging and discovered that a similar mistake had been made in the past. Since no real harm was done here, filing a revision report should be enough. And you only need the stamp from the counter chief, so no need for a report to headquarters. Make sure to get it tomorrow."

"Y-you've even looked up a past example?!" Laila cried out in shock.

Of course she would be surprised. Jade had pulled off a task of his own accord that Alina had yet to teach Laila.

Yes, the amazing thing about Jade was his ability to deal with issues with flexibility.

He'd thought to look into things on his own before asking someone about it, had found a problem that resembled his by searching through mountains of past documents, and had used that example to come up with a solution by himself. And he'd done all of this with transparency, making sure to report to Alina both before and after the incident.

It was highly vexing to admit, but Alina was so grateful to Jade for being able to manage during her overtime grind that she could call him a god.

"What the heck…? How is he so perfect at office work…?! It pisses me off how he can just be so useful out of the gate…!!"

Laila slumped beside Alina, who was gritting her teeth. "I've lost my confidence too, Alina…"

15

"…Laila, hey, Laila."

Jade lightly shook Laila by the shoulder. The newbie receptionist, whose face was planted on her desk, lifted her head with a "hmm?" Drool was dripping from the corner of her mouth, and wrinkles had developed on the quest form she'd used as a pillow.

"You can't take any more. You should go home and sleep. There's always tomorrow."

"…Wahhh, what about Alina? Ah, she's still at it…" Halfway through saying that, Laila looked at Alina's desk, saw that it was still piled high with documents, and got the picture. Alina had said she was going to get some air to wake herself up, and she wasn't there.

"We've got enough done," said Jade. "I can see the Centennial Festival ahead."

"Then I can feel okay about going home!" Happy as if she was going with him herself, Laila began efficiently getting ready to go. Just then, as she rustled around while tidying up the document-strewn desk, she murmured, "…Just so you know, Master Jade, Alina is actually really kind and strong."

"Huh?" He looked up at her.

Laila no longer had a sleepy expression on her face, and when their eyes met, hers were a little sad. "I mean, I'm told that she's been doing extra work on her own since she was a newbie, and even though she's suffered a lot, she still makes sure to stay with me while I do my overtime. She's not like, *I suffered, so you have to suffer, too!* You can't be like that unless you have a strong heart, right?"

"...I know that Alina is kind, too," Jade replied, vividly reminded of his memories from one month prior.

Tears had streaked down her face as he teetered on the brink of death. Her lips had been pressed tight, as if trying to hold something back, but her beautiful tears had spilled out regardless. She had cried for him, abandoning her overtime, her peace as a receptionist, and everything else to come save him.

He never wanted to see her like that again.

"It's startling how committed Alina is to being self-reliant. Someone like me will go straight to someone else for help, but no matter how much work she has piled up, no matter what happens, she forces herself to try to solve things on her own. She's so bad at asking other people for help that she wears herself down. That's why I'm surprised that she'd rely on you." Laila chuckled gladly—then suddenly dropped her eyes a bit and murmured, "Please support Alina... No matter what happens in the future."

"Huh? Yeah, I was planning on doing that anyway."

A shadow had fallen over Laila's face. Jade could only wonder for an instant why she looked so sad, as her earlier expression was immediately replaced by a bright smile.

"Well then, I don't want to intrude on your love nest, so I'm going home!" Laila beamed as if satisfied with Jade's response, then got ready and left Iffole Counter in the blink of an eye.

"..."

Alone in the quiet office, Jade sank into his chair and looked up at the ceiling. "...I've got to...get stronger..."

Sigurth skills. With his current powers, he couldn't go toe to toe with the dark gods, who used Dia skills. And that wasn't all—a tank who couldn't block the enemy's attacks was basically dead weight.

If only I had a Dia skill. Wicked thoughts flitted through his mind.

Only now could Jade understand how other adventurers felt, desperate in their desires for Dia skills. He never would have been able to empathize had he not learned of the advanced entities known as dark gods.

An unknown power was attractive. He felt like if he just had that, then he could resolve all his current problems. No—he could even feel himself falling for the delusion that he would never resolve this extraordinary problem without that kind of power.

But that's not right.

Before relying on some dubious skill that may or may not even exist, it was more important to take the small steps that he could take now. That was what Jade's master had taught him. That had never changed, even now that people called him the strongest tank in the guild.

"A way to beat Dia skills with Sigurth skills, huh…?"

The truth was that he had only come up with a single idea. Or rather, once, when he had been green and inexperienced, he had come up with the simplistic idea of a way to wield power greater than that of a Sigurth skill. But it was so dangerous that he'd nearly died when he actually tried it out, and his teacher dismissed the idea as "idiocy."

"…Guess I have to try it. That's my only option now."

16

She was dreaming.

Lululee was in a deep, dark forest, standing before two dead bodies.

One was a black mage. His entire arm, rod and all, had been

ripped off, and his neck was twisted in the wrong direction. The other was a swordsman, splayed over a tree root. His armor and stomach had been ripped open. His whole body was red with blood, and his eyes were empty.

"Why...?" The tank's voice trembled with resentment. He was missing his right arm, and his canines were bared. "Why didn't you heal us...?!"

He turned toward Lululee, revealing that the right half of his face had been gouged with painful-looking lacerations. His right ear had been lopped off, and his right eye had been gouged out, blood still gushing from it.

Lululee's face was pale with confusion, and all she could do was apologize. "I'm sorry, I'm sorry, I'm sorry..." She couldn't even attempt to make excuses for herself, like, *No, I did try to heal you properly. I did mean to save you. But this situation was hopeless...*

Aiden continued to blame her. "You're a—!"

Murderer.

The voice cursing her turned into that of another man.

She lifted her head with a start to find Aiden gone, a man with silver hair standing in his place. She knew him. He was their reliable leader, a man who cared for his allies.

But then, without any warning, his head fell off his shoulders with a *thunk*.

"Eek...?!"

That hunk of meat splattered on the ground, and beyond it lay more bodies.

That was the red-haired black mage who always teased her. And that was the receptionist girl who was always grumbling about overtime but was stronger than anyone.

"—!!"

These were all faces she knew, people she wanted to protect. But they were covered in blood and had stopped breathing.

Murderer.
I killed them.
I did—

****

There were three more days until the Centennial Festival.

With the major event fast approaching, people were already slowly starting to set up street stalls on the streets of Iffole. The decorations for the festival were already perfect, and if you didn't know better, it would seem like the festival could start any minute.

But as Lululee walked down the cheerful streets, her expression was heavy. The hustle and bustle of the city did not move her heart. She was too fixated on the awful nightmare she'd had that morning.

After walking silently toward the main gates of Iffole, Lululee finally made up her mind and spoke to Lowe, who was there beside her. "U-um."

"Hmm?"

"...You're not going to ask?"

"Ask what?"

"Um, about...um...me being a murderer..."

"Ahh."

He did remember Aiden calling her that the other day in the Forest of Eternity, but nobody had tried to ask about what he meant since. They were surely trying to be kind, but that just made it more painful for Lululee—to the point where she would have preferred if they interrogated her about it.

And so, unable to take it anymore, Lululee had brought it up herself.

But Lowe just stared idly at crowds on the street as he answered disinterestedly, "Not really. I don't care."

"..."

"I'm more worried about what our leader called us out for all of a sudden... I wonder, do you think he's gonna kick me out of Silver Sword because I'm too unmotivated?"

Lowe seemed so disinterested in her past that Lululee felt a little sullen about it, but she answered him seriously. "...He said it was special training."

"Huh? I didn't hear anything about that."

"He said he's going to be doing some especially dangerous training, so he wants us to be with him. You just weren't paying attention."

"Huh, for real? What's he trying to do this time...? And here I thought he was supposed to be bedridden for the next two months..."

"..."

It seemed he was genuinely indifferent about Lululee's past, from the bottom of his heart.

What the heck? Isn't that a little cold? Although she simmered with anger at the outrageousness of it, she was still scared to be questioned in detail, so she shut her mouth.

They passed through the main gates and came out onto the street. Unsurprisingly, the place was full of people coming and going to prepare for the Centennial Festival. As many people—merchants, travelers, adventurers, and their covered wagons—poured into Iffole one after another, Lululee and Lowe got into a carriage. They told the driver their goal was the guild headquarters, paid him, and were on their way.

Sitting opposite each other, Lululee and Lowe watched the scenery out the windows and remained silent. But just when they started to hear the clopping of hooves...

"What Aiden said was true!" Lululee cried out, finally leaping to her feet.

"Whoa, you startled me." Lowe, who had been gazing out the

window, widened his eyes at Lululee's abrupt declaration. "What's this about all of a sudden?"

"A long time ago, when I was still a beginning adventurer, Aiden was the tank in my first party! That was when I was a newbie, before my Sigurth skill manifested!" Lululee declared all in one breath, red in the face.

Her fear of having her past exposed had totally evaporated—now she just wanted Lowe to listen. No, that wasn't quite right—it was that hiding her past hurt more.

Now Lowe was the one getting flustered. "F-fine, fine, you actually want me to listen, right? I'll hear you out, so sit down, okay?"

"…" Cheeks puffed up in a pout, Lululee plopped herself back down aggressively on the seat as told, averting her eyes as she spoke rapidly. "I-it's not like I *want* you to listen…! Just, um, since I was called a murderer, I figured I have to offer a proper explanation…! Actually, wouldn't curiosity get the better of you at times like these and you'd ask me?! Why the heck are you ignoring me?! Do you hate me?! Are you that disinterested?! You better listen to my story!!" Lululee's feelings exploded at Lowe as she burst into tears with a *wahhhhh*.

Lowe froze, growing more and more startled. His reaction made sense. Even if Lululee did cry easily, the fact that she'd started yelling like a child all of a sudden was quite strange. Lowe thought of her as the most levelheaded person in the party.

"Uh, it's not like I was ignoring you," he said. "Leader and I avoided asking because we don't care what they have to say about yo—"

"I care!"

"I get it, so I'll listen, I'll listen. I mean—let me hear about it?"

"…"

While she felt rather miffed about being consoled like a child, Lululee took some deep breaths and then began telling her story in a low murmur. "…One day…our novice party reached a boss room faster than anyone for the first time. The dungeon didn't have many floors, so we were glad... And then we just went on ahead to challenge the floor boss without thinking."

The result had been a crushing defeat.

Their tank, Aiden, had been unable to hold the enemy's aggro, so the floor boss had started to target their attackers and Lululee. In the confusion of the battle, their frontline and ranged attackers had both been badly wounded. But Lululee hadn't manifested her Sigurth skill back then, and she hadn't been great at magic, so she didn't have the capacity to save both.

So she'd been forced to make a decision—to abandon one of her party members.

"But I just couldn't choose between them...so I healed both of them halfway..."

The time she wasted wavering over the decision resulted in a devastating outcome. Aiden had ended up losing his right eye and left arm, and their frontline attacker and ranged attacker both lost their lives.

"Ahh...I see, so that's what he meant when he called you a 'murderer.'" It seemed like Lowe got it, but his voice was still completely level.

"From Aiden's point of view, I wasn't able to fire off a single heal when my allies were in trouble, which cost him an arm. It's no wonder he calls me a murderer."

"...Hmm."

Lowe furrowed his brow, and he scratched at his red hair as he sighed. "That's like, well—maybe you weren't powerful enough. But if the party was falling apart to begin with, then the fault also lies with the tank for failing to hold aggro and the attackers for failing to overcome the enemy. But he's blaming it all on you? I'd be pretty put off if he honestly thinks that way."

"W...well, but it's still true that the healer has a lot of responsibility..."

"If you start arguing about who's responsible for a loss, it'll never

end. Even if party members die, you never make it anyone's fault…
That's the unspoken rule of adventuring. There's a limit to what
people can do. If you've got multiple bad conditions, then it doesn't
matter if you're a novice or a veteran, you'll still wind up dead. You
should be prepared for that as an adventurer."

"Th-that's true, but…," Lululee muttered under her breath, still
unconvinced. There were some things in the world that couldn't be
explained rationally. Lululee felt like she could understand Aiden's
feelings, in how he clung to being a tank even after losing an arm.

The way he saw it, he'd lost his eye and limb for unfair reasons.
You would need unimaginable strength in order to swallow all that
anger and resentment and move on. Aiden keeping on as a tank had
to be a form of revenge against Lululee.

"I'm nothing more than a healer with a powerful skill. On my
own, I'm worthle—," Lululee started to say before quickly shutting
her mouth. If she said something like that, then Lowe would know
that she was just a talentless healer with a fancy ability.

*A skill that continues to heal you automatically once it's conferred?
That's an amazing Sigurth skill.*

Jade had been startled by Lululee's skill after she'd introduced
herself on the day she was selected to be Silver Sword's healer.

But that was nothing new. Lululee manifesting *Sigurth Revive*
had completely transformed how people looked at her. People
would completely reevaluate her after she explained it, saying, *Wow,
that's amazing.* But Lululee hadn't been able to accept that praise.
She hadn't gained the skill through effort; God had just handed it
to her on a platter.

"…" Lowe watched Lululee for a while as she hesitated to speak,
then slowly reached over to rustle her hair.

"Wahhh?!"

"Well, if some loser can't stop bringing up the past and calls you
a murderer, don't worry about it. I believe more in what I've seen
you do than what he has to say."

"..." Hair still mussed up, Lululee looked down in silence for a while.

For a guy who was always flippantly cracking jokes, Lowe actually kept a firm eye on his allies—just like he had in that fight against the dark god a month ago. Maybe he'd picked up on all Lululee's worries.

But it seemed that he genuinely didn't care about what Aiden had said, in a good way. That was, in other words, also proof of the trust that Lululee had built with them as a member of Silver Sword.

So then she should just stop worrying and go on like she always did. There shouldn't have been anything to freak out about.

There shouldn't have been, but...

"Wh-what the heck?" Lululee sulked. "You're making it sound like I'm an idiot for worrying about this."

"Huhhh, so you worry about things?"

"I do!"

Lululee pouted, jerking her head away and puffing up her cheeks as Lowe cackled teasingly. This was so normal for them, it felt out of kilter.

"I do..."

But still—no, precisely because of how normal this felt—the murky feelings in her heart only amplified.

Is it okay for me to be here?

Wasn't it inevitable that she would betray her party members' trust and disappoint them someday? Her reunion with Aiden had thrown into relief the unease that had wormed its way into her head ever since their battle with the dark god. The more she thought about it, the deeper it dug in, spreading and swelling up.

"..."

But crying to Lowe about this any more than she already had would just be annoying. With a quiet thanks, Lululee shifted her gaze to the cold gates of the Adventurers Guild headquarters, visible from the window.

Wasn't it inevitable that she would become a murderer once more? Lululee was unbearably afraid of that…

17

Lululee and Lowe arrived at the guild headquarters and headed to the training grounds, as Jade had specified.

"I wonder what he means by dangerous training…," Lululee muttered, prompted by her anxiety.

Jade was a reliable guy, as both an adventurer and a tank, but at the bottom of his conviction was a genuine willingness to put his life on the line. That determination had made him the strongest tank in the guild, but as the party's healer, Lululee found the way he fought highly anxiety inducing.

"If he said it was dangerous, then it's gonna be dangerous…," Lowe responded. But judging by his almost exasperated expression, he had to be feeling as uneasy as Lululee. "Though he seems like a sensible guy, he really does have a few screws loose…in more ways than one."

Lowe's complaint was cut off by the sound of something bursting. At the same time, a red flash exploded from the courtyard area.

"…The training grounds?! Was that him?!" Lowe yelled and dashed off. Lululee hurried after him.

"Jade?!"

Jade was standing all alone in the wide training grounds.

Red lights swirled and swayed in the space around him, flickering and scattering purple lightning flashes. The lightning effect appeared when a Sigurth skill was activated. Jade must have been activating his skills, but Lululee had never seen the light spread out over such a wide area like this.

"Wh-what is going on…?" she murmured.

"Hey, you're here." Jade finally noticed the two of them and turned around. In contrast with the terrific phenomenon occurring around him, he had a serene look on his face. Lululee breathed a sigh of relief.

"Was that light coming from you, Jade? What were you doing…?"

"Special training." He waved his arm, and the red glow of the skill vanished. "I just thought up something… Ahh?" He tried to walk toward them, but then he suddenly fell to his knees. "Huh?"

Then gravity took him down the rest of the way and he fell on his face.

"Jade?!"

"Leader?!"

As Lululee and Lowe blanched, Jade, face down on the ground, muttered weakly under his breath, "I…I can't get up…"

18

""Activating multiple skills at once?!""

In the medical room of the guild headquarters, Lululee's and Lowe's voices both rang out at exactly the same time.

Seeing their reactions, Jade smiled wryly on his sickbed. He had figured Lululee would certainly get mad, but it was surprising that even Lowe had reacted so dramatically.

"Yeah, I thought that if I activated *Sigurth Wall* and *Sigurth Blood* at the same time, maybe I could raise my defensive capacity even higher than befo—"

"Are you an idiot?! Using multiple skills already places a huge burden on the user!!" Lululee barked at him without even hearing everything he had to say.

"Well, a long time ago, I just got the idea that maybe it'd be strong if I activated two skills at once… I guess it was dumb."

"I'll bring Alina into this!" Lululee cried. "I'll have her give you a nice wallop!"

"Heeeeey, Lululee! Don't—" Jade went white as a sheet and desperately tried to stop Lululee, who was about to dash off to call for Alina.

That was when someone with a cool, composed voice addressed him. "My, I was wondering what that ruckus was all about—so it was you, Jade."

A woman in a long white coat was standing at the entrance.

"Shelley!" Tears in her eyes, Lululee threw herself at the woman in the white coat—Shelley—the moment she saw her. "You tell him, Shelley! Jade's a stupid idiot!"

"Aw, no, did you make Lulu cry again, Jade?" While hugging Lululee to her ample bosom, Shelley turned her attention to Jade. Then she leaned right into him without any hesitation, pushing up his chin with a finger to begin examining him closely.

"Oh-ho, this looks like stage two of skill overuse backlash."

Shelley's beautifully shaped eyes, bordered by long eyelashes, were right there in front of him. She was a good-looking woman in her early twenties, with glamorous hair tied in a ponytail and an ample bust despite her exceptionally slender figure. But even under the gaze of Shelley, who was said to be one of the top five most beautiful women in guild headquarters, all Jade did was sigh.

Though she may not have looked it, she was the world's foremost expert on relics and a member of the guild's research team.

Shelley had created next-generation tools that applied relic technology, such as the guiding crystal shards and the holographic device. But though she was a capable woman, she was also a bit of an eccentric.

"For starters, there are stages to skill overuse backlash."

Shelley had not only researched relics out of a "personal interest," she'd also invested time and effort into studying skills. And now, she was breathing a large, exasperated sigh as she broke straight into a lecture.

"What is generally known as skill exhaustion—the notable feeling of full-body weariness and loss of strength after overusing your skills—is the mildest level of backlash. Go past that, and clear abnormalities arise in the body, such as loss of consciousness or sensory dysfunction. What comes next is clear pain, the final warning the body gives. If you push past this and continue to use your skills, you can sustain bleeding and organ damage. In the worst-case scenario, you can die from shock or blood loss."

"Wait, wait, wait." Jade rushed to stop Shelley from talking before Lululee could get anxious enough to start frothing at the mouth and roll her eyes back in her head. "C'mon, Shelley, don't scare us so much. I knew all that when I started."

While laughing innocently in a voice like tinkling bells, Shelley said something even more cruel. "Oh really? But if you're aware of it, and then hold out to even more severe skill exhaustion, it would make you an interesting subject for experiments… That's too bad."

"…"

Yes—she was a sicko who thought of Jade, with his high endurance, as an excellent subject for experimentation.

Before she could get any strange ideas, Jade changed the subject. "More importantly, Shelley, I came here on some business."

"Oh yes." She clapped her hands, then started to rummage around in a pocket of her coat as though she'd remembered what she was here for. "I found out something rather interesting from that thing you gave me a while ago, and I just reported it to the guildmaster. When I heard you happened to be here, I figured I'd tell you myself… Here," she said. Then she carelessly pulled out a shiny black stone the size of a clenched fist.

No, it wasn't just a stone. It was the heart of a dark god, which had been embedded in Silha, whom they had encountered a month ago in the White Tower.

"Whoa, whoa, whoa, whoa, you were just carrying something that deadly in your pocket?!"

As Lowe panicked, grabbing Lululee and hiding in the corner, Jade accepted the black rock. It had a significant heft. The surface of the stone was cracked where Alina had hit it.

"Did you discover anything about it?" Jade asked.

"It's clear that it's the heart of a dark god…yes. Or rather, it may be more accurate to call this a god's core—its main body."

"…Its main body?"

"Go on, take a closer look. It looks like a black rock, but it's not *colored* like that."

Jade did as he was told and gazed closely into the black rock—no, into the "god core."

The moment Jade saw it, he broke out into goose bumps. "—?!"

He just about flung the god core away from him before just barely managing to stop himself. He shifted his gaze toward the god core again, but he couldn't bring himself to examine it.

The "black" of the stone was stirring—that was the only way to describe the inside of the god core. It was disgusting, as though a whole bunch of winged insects were squirming around in there.

"Wh…what is this?" he stuttered.

"Those are all magic sigils."

"Magic sigils…?"

"If you keep writing characters on top of characters over and over again, the surface will turn entirely black, so you won't know what's written there anymore, right? There's an incredible number of magical sigils all smushed together in this god core, which is what makes it appear to be a solid color."

The term *magic sigil* reminded Jade of something. "Are those magic sigils the same ones that show up for Dia skills?"

When Alina activated her skill *Dia Break*, a magical sigil always appeared. Just like materializing weaponry, it was a phenomenon not seen with Sigurth skills.

"Most likely. It means there's an absolutely fantastic number of Dia skills packed into this god core. Basically, this thing is dangerous.

It's unlike any other relic I've analyzed before." You'd think this would be a grave thing to say, but Shelley sounded gleeful as she explained. "But that brings up a mystery. This god core has a whole bunch of Dia skills inside it, and the dark god Silha had it inside his body. But he only used three Dia skills, right?"

The tone of her voice rising even higher, Shelley continued on in excitement. "*Dia Storm*, *Dia Judge*, and *Dia Drain*... There's so much more information contained in the god core, but Silha only used those three. You'd assume he would be able to use all the skills in the god core, right? But even when the Executioner had him cornered, he stuck to those three skills. It's strange."

"True..."

"So then I came up with a hypothesis. It wasn't that the dark god didn't use Dia skills—it was that he *couldn't* use them. I figure there's conditions to drawing out skills from the cores."

"Conditions?"

"Yes. For example, it's possible that he can only draw as many skills from the god core as the number of people he's killed with his own hands—in other words, the number of souls he's eaten."

Jade widened his eyes. "That's right...all four members of Rufus's party died at the White Tower...but Rufus killed himself. And after offing the three other members of Rufus's party, Silha used three Dia skills... The numbers match up. The dark gods use human lives to power themselves, so it wouldn't be strange for there to be a close relationship there." And that wasn't the only thing. Silha had repeatedly referred to killing as "eating." "So does this mean the gods see humans as power sources for drawing out Dia skills...?"

"If this theory is correct," Shelley said, "then the more people a dark god kills, the more Dia skills they gain, and the more their strength increases. If a being like that came into town... Aww, geez, humanity would be wiped in no time flat!!" Despite having struck on such an unthinkable possibility, Shelley seemed enchanted with the subject of her research.

"..."

Seeing that Jade was exasperated, she chuckled and gave him a broad smile. "By the way, when I reported that to the guildmaster, he went just as pale as you are right now."

"Yeah, no wonder..."

"We really have to find that man in black quick, or things might get dangerous, hmm?"

"..."

The "man in black."

Jade frowned at the phrase that spilled carelessly from Shelley's lips.

They had gotten some information from Aiden after capturing him in the Forest of Eternity the other day. According to the results of the interrogation, he and his friends had never been in contact with Rufus—they'd gotten that information about Dia skills from a man in black whom they hadn't gotten a good look at. The way the guild understood it, it was highly likely that the man in black had told Rufus about dark gods.

"...The 'man in black,' huh...?"

They'd given information to Rufus and Aiden to make them pawns, while plotting the revival of the dark gods from the shadows.

Aiden had said that the man in black was like a ghost. Wearing jet-black robes like a burial costume, he had appeared suddenly, only to vanish just as abruptly right in front of them once he'd finished his business. And they hadn't learned anything about him, aside from that he had a low voice. After learning from the man in black about the special relic that could grant Dia skills, Aiden and company spread the story around and made adventurers search for secret quests, plotting to use them to find hidden dungeons.

"Maybe he really is a ghost who resents the world of the living?" Shelley suggested. "That's why he's like, *I'll revive the dark gods and destroy the world!* or something?"

"I'm not gonna let the world get destroyed by a ghost..." Jade heaved a sigh.

Agh, what a thing for the ancients to leave behind. He couldn't help but complain internally.

19

"A dark god, huh?"

They were in a special room on the highest story of the guild headquarters.

The floor was covered in an expensive rug woven of rare fur, and a heavy guard was posted at the entrance while the center of the room featured only a thick, circular craftsman-made table. This chamber, which was called the audience room, was rarely used.

There, Guildmaster Glen was down on one knee, gaze lowered as he answered:

"Yes, they are called dark gods."

Three other people were sitting around the circular table, but they were all a standing far above that of ordinary folks.

Two hundred years ago, the continent of Helcacia had been over-flowing with monsters. The first four people to land there and begin clearing it had been titled Swordmaster, Holy Mother, Guardian, and Sage. Together, these Four Saints were the forebears of all adventurers.

The four individuals in the audience room had inherited those bloodlines and were known as the fourth generation of the Four Saints.

The original saints were the founders of the Adventurers Guild, and though it went without saying, the fourth-generation saints were the head of the Adventurers Guild. While Glen, as guildmaster, had

the authority to manage the business end of things, he had to defer to the decisions of the Four Saints.

The Four Saints had built not only the Adventurers Guild but the human towns on Helcacia. This lineage had been watching over them for a long time. They were the absolute sovereigns of the Helcacia continent.

"The dark gods are fascinating, of course, but it's also truly interesting that secret quests really do exist." That remark came from one of the Four Saints. He was a man past middle age, with peaceful eyes and a long white beard—the fourth-generation Swordmaster.

Glen was delivering his annual report to the Four Saints. During this session, he had told them about the encounter with the dark god one month ago.

"How did the stories go? If you take on a secret quest, a hidden dungeon containing a special relic will appear...was it? Goodness, I took that for the sort of fantastical tales that adventurers would come up with for amusement. But to think that it was based in truth..."

"Do you know anything about secret quests?" Glen quietly asked the Four Saints.

The Four Saints represented the bloodline with the longest history on the continent. Their knowledge and techniques were taken as divine, and the secrets of their arts had been passed down in their line for two centuries. The knowledge they passed down included histories of the Helcacia continent that couldn't be widely publicized. If anyone knew of the truth of secret quests, surely it would be none other than the Four Saints.

But contrary to Glen's expectations, the Four Saints frowned at his question.

"Unfortunately, I heard nothing of secret quests when I inherited my predecessor's knowledge. Our ancestors established the quest system and were the first to administrate the exploration of dungeons. We saints should be aware of everything and anything related to quests—but what about you all?" The Swordmaster prompted the other two to respond.

"I've haven't heard of these secret quests, either," replied the fourth Guardian in a gentle voice. He was also of the fourth generation, like the older Swordmaster, but he was still a young man.

Despite having inherited the blood of the shield bearer from two hundred years ago, he was the complete opposite of his muscular, hairy predecessor. He had a slender frame and soft skin, and his face was as beautiful as a piece of art. He was a pretty man, the type who looked like he'd be blown away in a strong breeze.

"I assumed secret quests were tall tales, too," said the Guardian. "But to think that they're real, and there's even something as scary as dark gods slumbering there... If they were that big a deal, our predecessors would have made sure to tell us about them. So why didn't we hear about it? It's strange."

"I haven't heard a thing about that, either!" the lively voice of a child cut in, interrupting the Guardian's leisurely statement.

The fourth Guardian had inherited his title fairly early for a saint, but now there was someone among their number who was even younger.

"Even this cute li'l Holy Mommy's never heard of it. This story stinks something funny!"

This was the fourth-generation Holy Mother.

On one of the chairs generation after generation of saints had sat in, three cushions were piled on top of one another so the girl could just barely get her face over the table—she was that young.

The fourth Holy Mother was not yet ten years old, with long hair that fell to her waist, a determined slant to her eyebrows, and impactfully charming eyes that were like a doll's. Proud to finally be allowed to speak as one of the Four Saints, she shrewdly puffed out her chest atop her cushions.

"They didn't write about the dark gods in the *Libri*, either," she said.

"...I see," Glen replied.

The *Libri* was a book of the complete history of the continent, spanning from two hundred years ago, when the original saints had set foot on Helcacia, to the modern day. Every generation of saints had added to it, then passed it down to their successors.

"If it's not written in the *Libri*, then we're stuck, huh?" Glen commented.

"That cannot be said for certain!" said the Holy Mother. "The *Libri* we have now is incomplete. This is a matter of much serious business—besides, it's too quick to assume that we don't know anything about secret quests when only three of the saints have spoken. There's one more we haven't asked, isn't there?" the Holy Mother said a little sadly, gazing at an empty seat with no one in it. "I would like to hear the Sage's opinion. Though he doesn't look like anything special, he's the most knowledgeable of all of us and a passionate researcher! The fourth Sage might know something."

One of the four seats at the round table was currently empty.

The Sage, one of the fourth generation of saints, had vanished suddenly for no apparent reason without a word.

At the time, the world had been abuzz with theories of kidnapping or assassination, and the Adventurers Guild had sent out a fair number of people to search for his whereabouts, but in the end, they never found him. Not only were they unsuccessful at determining whether he was still alive or not, but they also hadn't even come up with a single reason as to why he would have vanished. Ten years had passed since.

The saints' conversation veered off the topic of hidden quests.

"Maybe we should do something about the Sage's empty seat, after all," said the Guardian. "Even if we don't know if he's alive or dead, should we have it be unoccupied forever? I mean, the Sage is actually who's worked on the *Libri* records for generations…"

"Don't be so hasty, Guardian," the Holy Mother cut in. "Ending the pure bloodline of the Four Saints to pick someone random would just be giving them the name of the Sage—there'd be no point!

Besides, there's no way a personage as great as him would just die in a ditch without leaving anything behind," she said emphatically.

The Guardian's brows dipped. "But still, the fact remains that there's been no news at all. Look at it from another angle—isn't it more unlikely that someone as great as the Sage hasn't given us any sign at all for over ten years?"

"So then are you saying that the Sage is dead?!"

"Calm down, Holy Mother." The Swordmaster chided the two of them. "Our job is to make decisions among the saints, and we determined Sage's disappearance would be handled with an empty seat as we await his return. Besides, now is not the time to talk about such things."

"..."

The Holy Mother hung her head remorsefully. *Thank you*, Glen thought, breathing a sigh of relief. As the Swordmaster had hinted, what he truly wanted them to be aware of now was the dark gods.

The Swordmaster must have noticed Glen's relief, as he gave him a kind look. "Well, don't give my student so much trouble—and that's that."

All the knowledge and technology the Four Saints possessed, including the *Libri*, was passed down exclusively to their successors. However, the Swordmaster's bloodline was a little different. They actively passed down their techniques outside the bloodline, so they could be useful to the next generation.

In other words, they took apprentices. And it was no secret that the fourth Swordmaster was Glen's teacher.

"Swordmaster, please refrain from intimating personal relationships in a professional setting. It's bound to be taken as collusion...," Glen pointed out timidly. It was forbidden to say the names of the Four Saints in the audience room. Their presences were symbolic—deified, in a way—and so it was rude to treat them as individuals.

Of course, this statement from Glen was also fairly risky, but the Swordmaster didn't seem bothered at all, since he smiled amiably in agreement. "Oh, of course. Pardon me... But it's about time we change these outdated customs, like calling each other by our titles. It's so suffocating."

Though they didn't say anything aloud, the Holy Mother and the Guardian seemed to agree, as they both gave big nods.

"Well, that's that. We'll forbid any further discussion of the Sage. Let's avoid getting derailed and confront the topic at hand—the existence of the dark gods." The Swordmaster narrowed his eyes, which glinted sharply, before he continued. "If we're to assume the worst based on what the guildmaster says...then it's fair to call this a danger to everyone who lives on this continent. We are bound to walk the same path as the ancients. This time, thanks to the Executioner, we were able to end matters without incident, but that was no more than a series of happy coincidences."

"Shouldn't we just defeat them?" The Guardian's bold and heroic proposition made Glen frown. "The Executioner slayed the dark god Silha on his own, didn't he? Then it seems like he could do the same for the other slumbering deities... What do you think, Guildmaster?"

"I couldn't say for sure if he'd win. I heard from the Executioner himself this time—he said he doesn't know why he even won."

Alina had actually told him she won thanks to "the power of resentment at having her overtime interrupted," but of course he couldn't say that. While mentally making that correction, Glen recalled what Alina had told him. Apparently, she and the dark god Silha had been completely even in terms of power at first, but Alina had eventually won out. Despite that, they hadn't discovered how she'd managed to defeat the dark god when they should have been evenly matched.

"...Hmm?" Hearing Glen's answer, the Guardian, who had been calm until then, lifted his brows slightly and narrowed his eyes. "Are you saying that...he won with powers beyond his own understanding?"

"That's what I mean. The Executioner went up against a dark god who had access to multiple Dia skills and whose body could repel Dia skills, yet he won with a Dia skill of the same level. You can call that nothing short of a miracle. I believe it's dangerous to rely on that."

"Who even is the Executioner anyway?"

And there it was. Though Glen had been expecting this question, he gulped regardless.

"Have you gotten so big for your britches that you won't even tell the Holy Mommy, Guildmaster?" The Holy Mother smirked.

"..."

Glen was caught between a rock and a hard place right now—between the absolute authority of the Four Saints and the violence of Alina's ultra-powerful killer skill.

If he told them who the Executioner really was, then Alina would be angry with him. She was sure to be mad, even if he was dealing with the Four Saints. No—what he was really scared of was not taking physical punishment from Alina but losing her trust, which would extinguish any hold he had on her.

Glen still needed her to work for him.

"I have a promise with the Executioner. Of course, if it's absolutely necessary, I will do what needs to be done, but so long as it's not, I wish to respect his wishes."

"And what are his wishes?"

"To live an uneventful life. It seems that he yearns for a life free of battle."

"Really? That's far different from what I imagined... I sometimes hear tales of the Executioner, and they say he's mad for battle," the Guardian pressed Glen, practically interrupting him. His eyes were sharper now—he must have been interested in the subject of the Executioner. "I hear he shows up unexpectedly in dungeons where adventurers have struggled to defeat bosses alone. And when the Executioner appeared in Iffole a month ago, he defeated a raid boss and never took the pay. That makes it sound like he's just in it for the fight…! And you say he wants to live peacefully? That doesn't make sense."

"Well…ah…he does get that way…if the conditions are right."

"The right conditions? Ahh, I see. Mm-hmm, mm-hmm… heh-heh-heh," the Guardian muttered like he was somehow glad, and then a few seconds later, he must have been struck by some intense flash of insight, as he abruptly widened his eyes.

"I understand what the Executioner really wants!!" he yelled out of nowhere, belying his pretty-boy image. Then he leaned forward eagerly, huffing with enthusiasm.

"When trying to protect someone dear to them, people will take up the sword and draw the bow. The Executioner has got to be that sort of fellow! You need no reason to fight when it's for the sake of those you would protect! But if you just seclude yourself in peace, then you can't protect those you love! What passion! Oh, what passion!!" The Guardian became more and more enthused as he went on, and by the end of his monologue, he was leaning backward with his feet on the table, both hands in fists thrust up to the sky.

"…"

Everyone else froze up at the Guardian's complete transformation, but he didn't even notice. For two hundred years, the generations of the Guardian's bloodline had valued passion and virtue in bearing a shield for their allies, and most of them had been men who both looked and acted hot-blooded. Yet it seemed that even this gentle-looking pretty boy couldn't fight his blood.

"That's basically what it means if he's not fighting for money or thanks! The Executioner is a man among men!!" the Guardian yelled, eyes blazing.

Then a voice came from the side like a douse of cold water. "Shut up, Guardian. You're getting too worked up."

"…"

The young Holy Mother's harsh remark snapped the Guardian

out of it and knocked him down a peg. He shut his mouth and dejectedly returned to a proper sitting position.

"My apologies. I let my excitement get the better of me." The Guardian stuck out his tongue cutely with a *tee-hee* to cover his embarrassment.

While Glen was still speechless, the Holy Mother broke into a big nod. "But the Guardian's point is perspicuous. My mother often told me that when your feelings for others are strong, even healing magic can sometimes bring about miracles beyond your power. I bet the Executioner's strong will summoned a miracle that led him to victory against this unknown god! How splendiferous!"

As the saints kept launching into the speeches, incredibly moved by the Executioner, all Glen could do was reply evasively. "………… Ahh, I guess…"

What motivated him—her, rather—was overtime.

Extra work turned her into a berserker. That was what made her take up her hammer and head out into dungeons. In that light, that mental switch she flipped was a lot more concrete than fluffy and indefinite "feelings for others."

"Now our discussion is getting derailed again." Clearing his throat with an *ahem*, the Swordmaster got them back on track.

"If the existence of the dark gods who defeated the ancients came to light, it would stir up unnecessary unrest in Iffole…no, in all the people who live on the continent. Major unrest is bound to turn into riots. We must handle this information carefully. On that point, it was an excellent decision to obscure their existence."

As the Swordmaster praised Glen's decision, his eyes shone with an even sharper light before he continued. "But it's also a fact that the Adventurers Guild should not be handling this matter alone. This knowledge should be shared with all the guildmasters—the Information Brokers Guild, the Smiths Guild—confidentially. Our technology is inferior to that of the ancients. We must come together, or we will never find our way out of this situation."

The Swordmaster gave Glen a fixed look. In his eyes was not the majesty of a king—it was the look one gave a beloved disciple who had grown from your teachings, rising to the position of guildmaster.

"I'll be counting on you going forward, Glen."

20

"This is the last of it, Alina!" Jade declared triumphantly as he handed over a stack of papers that he'd finished processing.

It was late the night before the Centennial Festival, in the offices of Iffole Counter.

"Huh?" Alina, who had been seriously engaged in counting documents, made a confused noise as she lifted her head. "...The last of it?"

"Yeah. This stack of quest forms is the final one. There's no more work left."

"...There's...no more work...?"

Alina must not have been able to believe what she was hearing as she looked around the office with a stunned expression. It was no wonder. A bunch of empty potion bottles lay on her desk where she sat—that night, the last before the Centennial Festival, was the final spurt, and she hadn't had the time to look around. She'd just been desperately making her way through the paperwork.

But the office looked completely different from a few days ago. Before, it had been as chaotic as a battlefield, but now it was tidied up, with the processed forms in a neat pile.

"Wh...whoa...?!" Alina stumbled out of her chair as everything hit home.

A beat later and she was on her knees, staring up at the ceiling and thrusting both fists high as she screamed, "It's oveeeeeeeeeerrr!!"

After she howled for a while, Alina's eyes were a little moist, and her voice was trembling with extreme emotion. "I...I thought it would never end...! W-wah...ahh... Thank you, God...!"

"I guess it helped that the number of quests for processing lately has decreased. Besides"—rotating his stiff shoulders, Jade smiled with satisfaction as he continued—"this year's Centennial Festival has no special bonus period, right?"

"Yes, exactly!!" Alina replied, eyes flashing aggressively as she peeled off the document that was stuck on the office message board. Written in large characters on the notice the guild head-quarters had sent to the receptionists was the following message:

Notice of the cancellation of this year's Centennial Festival bonus period.

They listed out some plausible-sounding reasons for the cancellation: That it was to quiet down the inappropriate quest rush that had occurred due to the rampant rumors, that it was out of consideration for the danger of these unknown secret quests, and whatnot—basically, the guild was penalizing adventurers for repeatedly ignoring their warnings and running out of control.

"Heh...heh-heh-heh-heh...if there's no bonus, then nobody's going to bother trying to register a quest on the day of the Centennial Festival... I've won... This is a total victory...! God loves me...!"

"Yeah. Now you won't have any overtime on the day of the festival."

Despite the implementation of the penalty, the number of people who sincerely believed there was a relic that could get them a Dia skill had decreased at this point, and it was turning into something to laugh over. Apparently, some of the guild's leaders had been against canceling the bonus because things were settling down anyway, but Glen had pushed it through using his authority as the guildmaster.

As soon as Alina found out it was over, she immediately finished the day's totaling and said, "Then let's go, Jade!" like it was obvious what she wanted to do.

She spent just a few more seconds getting ready before she started to lock up Iffole Counter.

"Huh? Go where?" The dumb-sounding question popped out of Jade's mouth.

And then he got back a response he never would have expected. "Isn't it obvious? Since we've emerged from the clutches of overtime hell, there's just one thing to do—drink!!"

"............................Huh?"

For a second, he couldn't believe his ears.

Jade blinked twice, mouth hanging open as he went over what Alina had just said to him. Eventually, he put two and two together.

"Whaaaaaaaaaaaaat?!"

Now it was Jade's turn to cry out in surprise.

But of course, it was an invitation from Alina. The thing he'd thought he would never see in a hundred years had just plopped into his lap.

"Huh? Am I dreaming? Normally you would be like, '*Okay, bye*,' and just go straight home, right...?! Am I going to die tomorrow?!"

"If you're not coming, I'll go by myself."

"I-I'm right behind you!" Jade answered without hesitation, and he and Alina headed out into the late-night city.

21

The audience with the Four Saints had been weighing on Glen for the past few days, but now that it was over, he returned to his office, exhaustion on his face.

A woman relaxing on the guest couch greeted him. "Ah. Hello

there, Glen. Aww, nooo, you've gotten older again?" she said rudely as soon as she saw him, giggling.

Glen openly scowled at her laughter. "Why are you here this late at night, Jessica...?" He breathed a long sigh but nevertheless reluctantly sat down on the sofa opposite the guest couch.

Jessica was a brown-skinned woman with beautifully wavy hair that went to her shapely waist, and she was currently wearing an outfit that exposed her thighs. A gleeful smirk twinkled in her eyes when she saw Glen's annoyance.

"Oh my, you don't have to look so aggrieved the moment you see me. That's no way to treat the Information Brokers Guildmaster when she's come all this way to see you."

"I know we go way back, but nothing good ever comes of it when you come over. Just get your business done and leave."

"So cold! Jessie's gonna sulk."

"..."

"Tee-hee, I'm joking. I came for work today—W-O-R-K!" No sooner had she said this than she brought out a book and tossed it on the desk with a *ta-daa*.

"A book...? ...No, this is...!" The moment Glen laid his eyes on it, his exhaustion evaporated, and he rose instantly to his feet.

Jessica seemed quite satisfied by his reaction. "Aww, that sure changed your tune!"

No wonder—the cover of the book she'd brought him was inscribed with golden characters.

Those characters appeared to have been carved into the binding after the fact, as they weren't quite printed correctly and touched the spine of the book. Such a strange article could only lead to one thing:

"A secret quest...?! Where did you get that?!"

"Information broker" referred to someone who handled information for a living.

They sought out the rarest and most valuable knowledge, aggregated it, and sold it for a price to those who needed it. And the Information Brokers Guild, which supervised these brokers, amassed all sorts of intelligence.

But this was unexpected.

As Glen pressed her for an answer, Jessica made an X with her two index fingers right in front of his nose. "An information broker's duty to remain confidential is *absolute*! All I'll say is that it was from my super top secret route. ♡"

Glen finally regained a bit of composure as he leaned deeper into the sofa. "...You mean to say that a secret quest...won't necessarily be hidden in a relic?"

One month ago, Alina had discovered a secret quest by breaking a red orb relic, which caused the White Tower to appear. Relics were the hardest known substances, so without ungodly superhuman strength like Alina's, it would be unlikely you would destroy one relic physically, making it an optimal hiding spot. For that reason, Glen had thought for sure that future secret quests would be sealed away.

"That's what it looks like. I'd assumed that they were hidden in relics, too, so I was surprised."

"It looks like the quest hasn't been taken yet."

According to Jade, when you took a secret quest, golden characters would fly up, then vanish after you accepted. If you could see the golden characters, then it had yet to be taken. The hidden dungeon had yet to appear.

"Yep. I wanted to try taking it myself out of personal intellectual curiosity, but it seems that an information broker can't accept it, so it's no better than a piece of junk to me." Jessica folded her long legs the other way and gave a bewitching smile. "You want it, don't you?"

"...How much?"

"You're making it so easy for me! You'll take my asking price, right? Right? If you don't accept it, I'm giving it to another big spender. ♡ There's lots of people who want this, after all."

Jessica smiled devilishly and then stated her price.

22

"N-nobody is open..."

Alina gazed in shock at the main street. It was silent, populated only by the streetlamps that shined here and there.

"All the taverns are closed?!"

Alina had dashed out of the office in a post-overtime mood, taking Jade along with her to get drinks, only to happen upon this cruel sight.

Iffole, the city of adventurers, had many taverns, and they were frequently patronized. If there were customers, then they would stay open until dawn, and no matter how late at night it was, you could hear drunken laughter from one or two of them.

"...I guess it's not surprising that all the bars are getting ready for the Centennial Festival tomorrow," said Jade.

"No way...!" Alina's legs buckled, and her knees hit the cold flagstones. "This isn't right... This isn't right... I worked harder than anyone in Iffole, and I can't even get a refreshing drink after all that overtime...," she murmured in despair. Jade fell into a pensive silence beside her.

Then he suddenly took Alina by the arm and made an offer. "Let's swing by my usual haunt, then."

"Your haunt?"

Finding something about that word irritatingly quirky, Alina furrowed her brow.

Jade said proudly, "They'll definitely still be open. You want to drink, right?"

"…"

It was annoying, but she did indeed want a drink. Or rather, she wanted to savor this feeling of release. Well, so long as she could get her hands on some alcohol, Alina was fine with anywhere this time around. She reluctantly agreed, and Jade started walking in the opposite direction of the tavern-lined road.

"Huh? That way is where all the bars are, though."

"It's the opposite way."

Eventually, they reached the end of a narrow alley, then went down some stairs into a basement. At the bottom was a little door with a single light over it that hadn't been visible from the outside.

"'Noct Bar'? Huh, I never knew there was a tavern here." Gazing at the little sign in front of the establishment, Alina tilted her head. The place wasn't trying to draw in customers by being flashy. The entrance and sign were tucked away, as if the tavern didn't want anyone coming in.

"This is the tavern Silver Sword has used since way back."

There was a pleasant tinkling of bells as Jade entered, and then he was welcomed by the older man behind the counter.

"Oh, it's Jade. Welcome."

Catching sight of Alina coming in after him, the old barman widened his eyes slightly. Then he chuckled and grinned. "Is that your girlfriend?"

"No."

Seeing Alina immediately deny being the girlfriend to the handsome and famous adventurer Jade without even any change of expression, let alone a blush, the barkeep figured out what was going on and fell silent.

But Jade, who had a spirit of steel, fidgeted rather gladly as he gave an exaggerated shrug. "Heh…so finally, our relationship has gotten out…"

"Hey, could you not try to complicate things…?"

"It's all right. Of course, once people find out about us, I'm prepared to take responsibility and marry you."

"..
Uh-huh."

"I make some pretty good money, you know. Even on the off chance that you lose your job, I'm confident I could support you for your whole life! So don't worry and let's—"

Jade was cut off halfway with a *mgk*. Glassy-eyed, Alina smacked her right hand over his mouth to keep him from finishing his sentence.

"Mrmg?"

"Just *who* the *hell*..."

"Mmmf?!"

"...would ever get supported by someone like youuuuuuu?!"

"Mph!"

Slamming into the pretty floor of Noct Bar with a *bonk*, Jade rolled his eyes back in his head as he lay there spasming.

"..."

The barman gave the scene a few glances as he made an effort not to avoid Alina's gaze; she glared back at him.

"Barkeep...you saw nothing tonight. You got that?"

"...W-well, this was originally a place for members of Silver Sword to come in secret. I'm obviously not going to butt into matters between customers or carelessly disclose any information."

"Noct Bar has been around for a long time. I can guarantee you he doesn't have a loose tongue. Let's relax and drink, Alina." Revived like it was nothing, Jade sat down at the counter and prompted her to sit beside him.

Giving a sulky pout, Alina sat down, leaving an empty chair between them.

"Are you okay with grape wine, Alina? And I guess I'll order some food—oh, I'll let you handle the order, barman."

"…" Alina glared at Jade as he quickly and adroitly got the ordering done. "You're pretty used to this."

"You think so?" Jade gave her a puzzled smile. "Well, I *am* the leader of Silver Sword. I often go out drinking with guild management. When I'm with the upper ranks, I'm the youngest, so I end up doing this sort of thing a lot. Guess it's automatic for me."

"…?! Whoa…!" Noticing something with a start, Alina stood up from her counter seat.

I've been thinking that he's so smooth at everything here, but has he even mastered alcohol-based communication?!

Alcohol-based communication—a tricky skill but arguably one necessary for a career.

Pouring drinks for one another and talking openly filled in the invisible divide between superiors, coworkers, and underlings, fostering an environment where you could all work smoothly. It was a high-level adult technique.

Many were unskilled at alcohol-based communication and privately grumbled about how unnecessary it was—but that didn't change the fact that you would have to deal with it when you got a real job. And the real nasty thing was that you could only improve in this skill through real-world experience.

Once everyone's in their seats, Jade just checks with everyone about their drinks while he picks out the snacks—an aggressive ordering technique to keep things from dragging on and go straight to the toast… One wrong step, and it's bound to be taken as an uncomfortably forceful move, but he pulls it off so naturally…?! He must be very experienced…!

By the way, Alina was extremely bad at this, so when drinking with coworkers, she avoided danger by using the ultimate secret technique of automatically refusing everything but the bare minimum. In doing so, she'd garnered a reputation as someone who wouldn't join her colleagues even when invited.

That was because at the end of the day, the stress of having to deal carefully with coworkers while drinking was greater than the merits that could be earned through alcohol-based communication. There were a number of unavoidable social events out there, though, such as year-end and New Year's parties, send-offs and welcome parties, and seasonal gatherings.

"You seem like you'd hate this sort of thing from the bottom of your heart," said Jade.

"...Why are you even an adventurer...?"

Jade seemed like he could deal with social organizations better than Alina ever could—it kind of pissed her off, so she scowled.

Alina's family ran a tavern in a small town. The place had always been overflowing with local adventurers, and ever since she was little, she had watched big and strong adventurers who lived worlds away from white-collar notions like "alcohol-based communication." She'd always seen them as the types to be drunk before they even entered the tavern, not caring whether the booze and food came out as they'd ordered it, drinking themselves into a stupor, and scarfing down meat amid jeers of laughter and animated tales of adventure.

"If you're thinking we don't need these social skills since we work in the world of individual meritocracy, I'm afraid you're dead wrong."

"Really...? I was under the impression that adventurers were creatures who were drunk from start to finish."

"Well, I won't deny that... But you want to let loose when you're at a tavern, at least, when you're an adventurer."

"..."

Jade's nonchalant answer made Alina think back to her childhood.

To the adventurer she'd been closest with when she was little—a young man named Shroud.

He had put on a tough act and had liked to sit alone at the counter seats, insisting men had to be lone wolves. Yet his friends and acquaintances would always end up messing with him, forcing Shroud to drop the cool-guy act and burst into laughter. Alina had enjoyed that, too. There hadn't been any hassles like alcohol-based communication or suffocating working life at the tavern—just the preposterous dreams that the adventurers had talked about, and infinite exploits ahead of them.

Like Jade had said, maybe adventurers let loose like that in the taverns precisely because their career forced them to face a brutal reality: Death was never far from your side in dungeons.

Even Shroud, who always seemed so carefree, had lost his life on a quest. Adventuring was a profession synonymous with such abrupt ends.

"Besides, I actually kind of enjoy showing that kind of consideration," said Jade.

"Y-you like it?! You're so weird…!"

"Keeping an eye on the big picture at a party while also picking up on anything off, constantly using your head thinking about what to do next—that's what tanks do."

I see—so he's a born coordinator.

"…Well, anyway, let's toast to celebrate the end of overtime." With a sniffle, Alina pulled herself together and held up the mug she'd been offered. "I'm gonna live it up at Centennial Festival tomorrow…!"

"Yeah!"

Making a pleasant clanking sound, Alina and Jade struck their mugs together.

****

"But still…why is it always me…wahhhh, *hic*… The world is so unfair…"

Less than an hour after that cheery toast, Jade was rubbing Alina's back as she whined to him, thoroughly drunk at his side.

"You sure are a lightweight, Alina…"

For someone who had started drinking so aggressively, Alina was face down on the counter by the time she emptied a single mug.

Well, they said that alcohol got to you faster when you were tired, so perhaps she wasn't operating at full capacity.

"It seemed like she was pretty exhausted," said the barman.

Accepting the water the barkeep offered him, Jade held the mug carefully, shaking Alina's shoulder as she snoozed away. "Drink some water, Alina, then we'll head home. Can you get up?"

When he addressed her, Alina lifted her head. Exhausted from continuous overtime, she stared at Jade in a daze, cheeks flushed from liquor for a while. Just then...

"Shroud?" she muttered.

"Huh?" Jade was momentarily startled to be called a name he'd never heard before.

But it seemed that Alina believed that Jade was someone called Shroud. She latched onto his arm. "Shroud... What the heck? What a relief... You came back..."

"Hey." Jade's mind went completely blank for a moment, but then he got his bearings. By the time he realized what was going on, he was grabbing Alina by the shoulders. "Heeeey, who is that?! A guy?! Is that a man's name?! Who the hell is he?!" He pressed her for an answer, ignoring the very kind look the barkeep was giving him that seemed to say, *Oh, too bad for you.*

But she didn't answer, wearing the happiest smile he'd ever seen on her. "Shroud...you know...I became a receptionist..."

"L-like I said, who the heck is—?"

"I'll always be waiting...for you to come take a quest from me..."

"...!" Jade froze up as he listened to Alina's delirious ramblings.

Then she dozed off again. Watching her peaceful sleeping face, Jade struck on a certain possibility.

Despite having the incredible power of a Dia skill, Alina didn't even consider a change in career. Even though it was clear to anyone that she'd have guaranteed success if she became an adventurer, she was fixated on being a receptionist.

Could it be the real reason for that was...

"…Are you waiting for this Shroud person…?"

Jade got the now silent woman on his back. The barkeep took pity on him and said he didn't need to pay, but Jade forced the man to take the money and left Noct Bar late that night.

23

After Information Brokers Guildmaster Jessica left, Glen sat alone in the office, gazing silently at the book he'd just acquired—no, the secret quest.

Then came a sudden knock at the door. After waiting for Glen's response, his private secretary Fili came in.

Her face was expressionless and dispassionate as usual. She wore functional silver-framed glasses, her hair was neatly tied back without one strand out of place, and her uniform was crisp. She didn't so much as raise a brow when she looked at the secret quest in Glen's hands, adroitly tidying up the silver cup that Jessica had drained.

She was not only his private secretary, but a first-class bodyguard entrusted with protecting the guildmaster. She would never make any comment on the behavior of the man she guarded, and she had a full command on keeping personal emotion and sentiment from interfering with this.

"What will you do about that tome?" she asked.

"I'm putting it in the deepest layer of the underground labyrinth—in the underground book storage. I'm heading there now."

"Understood. I will make the arrangements right away, so please wait here." That was all Fili said before she left the office.

"…But damn…"

Listening to the sound of Fili's footsteps grow distant as he was left alone again, Glen scratched his head. He sighed as he stared down at the golden glow of the book in his hands.

The slightest of smiles played at his lips. "I can't believe she found one this easily."

He was grateful that Jessica had come to negotiate with the Adventurers Guild first. Well—this was the fruit of continuing to be the number one client of the Information Brokers Guild and maintaining a carefully built relationship with them. Occasions like these were why the Adventurers Guild kept in the Information Brokers Guild's good graces.

"They dug this up in no time flat. Information brokers sure are top notch these days… They're way more useful than those adventurers who fell for that rumor at least."

He'd anticipated this would take a while longer, though. Had someone really found it by chance and then sold it off to an information broker for a hefty sum? Honestly, he would have preferred it if an adventurer had discovered the thing and taken the quest themselves. That way, Glen could have avoided being ripped off by Jessica. Oh well.

"…I've found a secret quest. Now there's just the dark god to deal with."

The sulky frown of a girl rose in his mind—that of a particular receptionist, who was looking forward to the Centennial Festival.

The event would kick off tomorrow. The gods truly must have hated that girl for a secret quest to be found now, of all times.

"Looks like we'll be counting on you again, li'l miss."

24

That night, the city of Iffole was lit red. It was already overflowing with people.

Alina was standing in the square in front of the main gate, at the street entrance. She was wearing her unremarkable dress as per usual, but her expression sparkled like that of a young maiden with dreams as she fidgeted with her already-tattered guidebook.

The day she'd been waiting for had finally arrived; it was time for the Centennial Festival.

"...Wow...!"

The center of the festival, the main road, was already packed with rows of street stalls and filled with people. Delicious smells hung around them, and even though it was late, the area was bustling and lively, the light of the street stalls attacking the darkness of night. The full scene hit Alina like a wave, filling her field of view.

"I-it's starting...!"

Restraining herself from getting too excited over how fun the festival atmosphere was, Alina stared at the clock tower.

The clock tower was done up for the occasion, lit dramatically with magical balls of light. The thick minute hand eventually reached the peak with a tock, and the moment it struck six in the evening:

The *ta-tada-taaaa* of a trumpet echoed grandly through Iffole.

At the same time, magic lights that had been prepared beforehand were launched into the air. They burst and scattered gloriously with a sound that rumbled in the pit of her stomach, and the sky over the main way was filled with a giant flower of light. But the particles of light did not disappear; instead, they drifted down to the ground like snow. Then the festival decorations that had been set up on the main road also flicked on, transforming the daytime festival into a nighttime spectacle.

And with that dramatic show—the first night of the Centennial Festival had begun.

"Wooow! Wooow!"

Alina's previously haggard face burst into sparkles. The light returned to her eyes, which had been dead from exhaustion these past few days, to blaze brightly like jewels. The wrinkle that had constantly furrowed in her brow relaxed into an expression of joy, and her stiff cheeks flushed—now her face really did look very like that of a seventeen-year-old girl.

The scene she'd longed for all this time had unfolded before her eyes.

At one point, this event had seemed so close yet so far. Really far. The journey here had been long, and before all this, she'd wondered why she had to suffer so much. But now, it was finally in reach.

The Centennial Festival of her dreams!

"H-hurry! Let's hurry and go, Jade!"

There was no reply. When Alina turned around, she found Jade was standing there like he'd been struck with a petrifying curse, mouth hanging half-open as he stared at her. After a few seconds of immobility, he suddenly flopped over and fell backward.

"Wh-what...?" Alina stuttered.

Had all that overtime actually taken it out of him? Figuring something was up, she examined Jade—but he had a peaceful smile on his face, like that of a man passing away after living out a full life, hands folded in front of his chest as he let out a sigh.

"Ah...I'm just, wow... I feel like I could die without regrets after seeing that smile on your face..."

"..."

"That's right! You really are an innocent girl...! You've just lost a little of that quality from the exhaustion of overtime and the daily grind... Deep down, you're totally cute...!"

"...Sh-shut up." Belatedly remembering how giddy she'd just acted, Alina snapped out of it.

But though she barely managed her usual sullen look, she still couldn't restrain her excitement for the festival, and once Jade was on his feet, she tugged at his sleeve. "Stop babbling like an idiot and let's go already. We don't have all night. I—I want to repay you as soon as possible for buying my drinks yesterday and taking me home, so today is my treat."

"You really don't have to worry about it."

"I don't want to be in your debt!"

Eyes sharp, she gazed at the bustling festival. "I'm going to conquer this whole festival!!"

25

As the grand Centennial Festival got into full swing...

Lululee was walking along a cold, dark stone hallway.

"Hey, Lulu. Today's the day of the fun, fun festival...so why are we in this damp and dangerous underground prison?" muttered Lowe wearily, walking beside her.

Despite his complaints about how he wanted to be at the festival, Lowe was properly attired in his mage robes with his rod at his waist, ready to go into battle at any moment. Lululee was also fully equipped, just the same as when she went into a dungeon. But they weren't in one right now.

"I-if you don't want to do it, then you don't have to follow me!"

They were in an underground prison in a forest a short distance away from guild headquarters.

Just like the guild headquarters, this place had been constructed out of an underground labyrinth that had once been an S-rank dungeon.

There were thirty-four levels in total, with an underground prison for containing dangerous prisoners made on the tenth level. It had taken over fifty years to clear this dungeon, and it was said that even just totaling up the quest records, over ten thousand adventurers had fallen challenging this underground labyrinth—it was a literal maze of evil.

"You're the one who chose to follow me," said Lululee.

"I mean, I got worried, since you said you were going to meet

Aiden… Besides, if you bothered to tell me, doesn't that mean you wanted me to come along?"

"N-n-n-no!"

He was not wrong—in fact, it was exactly as Lowe said, but the fact he was spot on upset Lululee. She furrowed her brow in a scowl. "Enough! You should just go to the festival alone!"

"Fine, fiiiiine, don't sulk. I'll go with you."

"P-please don't treat me like a child!"

Sweeping aside Lowe's arm as he scrubbed roughly at her head, Lululee puffed up her cheeks in a pout. But she really did want him to come with her, so she said no more and changed the topic.

"…Apparently, it usually takes one or two weeks to get permission to enter the underground prison, though…"

To see someone who'd been sent to the underground prison, you'd normally write a justification for your visit and present it to the Adventurers Guild. It would need a review from the relevant team, stamps from all the various team supervisors, and the stamp of permission from the guildmaster and everything, so getting permission for an audience took quite a while.

"The guildmaster said that since the headquarters is so busy with the festival today, I can get permission from the other supervisors after the fact… I'll go to the festival tomorrow. So…" Squeezing Lowe's robe in her hand, Lululee muttered, "Forgive me for today…"

"…"

Lowe scratched his head and sighed. "So what are you gonna talk about when you see Aiden?"

"…"

"I doubt you can have a decent conversation with a guy who sincerely believes that his party wipe is purely the fault of the healer, though."

"…I know. But I can't help but think…that if I had managed to make the right choice then, or if I'd already manifested my Sigurth skill, then nobody would have died... I wasn't able to do anything in our fight against the dark god, either..."

Seeing Lululee bite her lip, Lowe sighed. "Man, it sure sounds like a drag to have a healer personality... I'll go with you—but I won't cut in, no matter what you talk about, and I won't help you, either. Got it? I'm a completely unrelated third party. That okay with you?"

"I-I'm fine with that!" Lululee's tone of voice was light with relief.

Turning his face away, Lowe muttered into thin air, "Hey, Lululee."

"What is it?"

"No matter what happened to you in the past, we're your friends now. None of us think of you as useless, and we definitely don't consider you a murderer—you better not forget it."

"!" Lululee's breath caught.

Lowe had said this curtly, without looking her in the eye, but it was gentler and warmer than anything. Lululee was glad she had a friend who would still say that, even knowing her past mistakes.

But even though that was true, even knowing that was how she should feel—Lowe's words still stabbed deeply into Lululee's heart.

Ahh, he was so kind.

He was so kind and talented; it was wasted on someone as dishonest as her. He was coolheaded, too, and had good judgment. She felt even more pathetic about how she was dragging things out, about how she couldn't let it go.

Lululee understood just as well as Lowe did that there was no point in dwelling on the mistakes of the past forever, and no matter what she said to Aiden, he wouldn't say what Lululee wanted him to, and it was wrong to seek forgiveness from him in the first place. She knew all that.

But her heart just couldn't be convinced. She wanted to be forgiven. She wanted to apologize, at least. She wanted it for her own selfish satisfaction. Her inexperienced heart raged with it, and she couldn't control it.

Lululee really was a dishonest person. She was completely unsuited to being a healer.

"…"

That dark god.

He'd stolen all her healing abilities when they faced off against him, leaving her completely useless. If Alina hadn't come to save them, everyone really would have died.

Lululee's friends saw her as a talented healer, but they didn't realize that without her skill, she was talentless. She prayed they would never catch on. She wanted to maintain that beautiful illusion—

—until it was all over.

"…Thank you for everything, Lowe."

"Huh? Did you say something?"

"It's nothing."

Once the Centennial Festival ended, she would lay down her rod. Lululee had made up her mind.

After the event drew to a close, she would tell the guildmaster that she was resigning from adventuring, from healing, and from Silver Sword.

She'd lost all confidence in herself after the battle with the dark god. If she said something appropriate, like *I can't bear this burden*, and put on a dejected look, then her friends should understand. They were kind, so they would understand how she felt. *And I'm going to take advantage of that kindness.*

While they're desperately trying to get stronger to face the dark gods, I'm going to leave them behind and run away. Surely, at the bottom of their hearts, they would be terribly disappointed in her.

But I'll be fine. Because I'm dishonest. Because it's way better for them to think that I've run away rather than for them to someday realize that I'm worthless.

The day they realized Lululee had no talent would be the day the whole party died. Before that happened—before it was too late—she would have them find a more talented, composed healer, who would make sure to save them when they were in trouble.

Biting her lip, Lululee forced back tears.

"Let's go, Lowe. If we can get this done quick in five minutes, then we can go to the festival!" Lululee said, forcing a smile.

****

They arrived at the first level of the underground prison. They went further in and eventually reached an open area. This chamber had once housed a floor boss, but now there was just a single surly jailer standing there alone. Lululee took one look at him and gulped.

This was the watchman of the underground prison.

He was short and stout but large, clad in armor emblazoned with the guild crest, and holding a giant ax.

As if to say, *I am a servant of law and order*, he didn't so much as raise a brow as he stood there, still as a statue, even as two members of Silver Sword walked in. When they informed the jailer of the situation, he demanded no permit from them, prompting Lululee and Lowe to move to a different room. The guildmaster must have pulled some strings on their behalf.

There was one little thing in the room they walked into—a crystal gate, glowing faintly red.

Crafted from a relic, the crystal gate could move things between other gates in the blink of an eye. However, the more broadly known crystal gates were made of blue crystal, while the ones in the underground prison were red crystal gates. These were special crystal gates that would operate only with the permission of an authority figure.

"Use this to jump," he said before returning to his post.

The underground prison had once been the subterranean maze of an S-rank dungeon, so it was convoluted to navigate. On top of that, the ancients had implemented technology here that made the hallways switch randomly. So the guild had made slow progress through the maze by setting up crystal gates in various locations.

The jails on the tenth level could never be reached by walking, and even now, getting around in the underground prison was done using the crystal gates that were left over from the cleaning period.

Lululee held a hand out over the red crystal gate, and with that familiar floating feeling, everything around them transformed.

Ahead of them lay a cold, dark, and claustrophobic stone pathway. Having swallowed ten thousand adventurers, this underground prison felt like it would send a shiver down your spine, right to the bone. A heavy feeling settled in around them, too heavy and imposing to have emanated from the bleak stone construction alone.

"..."

Without noticing she'd been grabbing Lowe's robe the whole time, Lululee swallowed her spit, automatically heading for the cell that was her destination.

26

"...Aiden." Lululee gently touched the cold metal bars with her hand. When she called out to the one-eyed, one-armed man sitting in the cell, he shot her a merciless glare.

"Ha, come with your buddy to show me pity?"

He looked at her like they had never been friends. It made Lululee flinch for a moment. A step behind her, Lowe folded his arms as he watched carefully.

"...I'm so—"

I'm sorry.

Lululee almost said it. *I'm so sorry I couldn't save you and everyone else back then.*

But now that she was actually here, it was like the words were stuck in her throat and wouldn't come out. She suddenly realized an apology like that would be selfish. Even if she had done what she could at the time, someone who had failed to save their allies had no right to apologize. It was too selfish, too cruel to say it just because she wanted to be forgiven.

"…"

Lululee ultimately found herself at a loss for words, and Aiden snorted at her. "Do you really think that I was stooping to this kind of shameless crime from the start?"

"Huh…?"

"After I lost everyone, I tried to get stronger the honest way. I believed that one day, I would manifest a skill that would let me go back to tanking, even with one arm… But then, I heard some news—a healer with a Sigurth skill named Lululee Ashford had joined Silver Sword."

"!"

"The girl who'd killed her party members had so *conveniently* manifested a Sigurth skill and was calling herself an elite adventurer? Ha-ha, ha-ha-ha-ha! What a riot, right?! How stupid I was, believing that I could still be a tank with one arm, making such piddling progress without a skill to my name!"

Aiden's eyes were wide, and Lululee could almost swear he was crying.

"Suddenly, I just didn't care anymore. No, it got me past it all, actually. I realized I had to take whatever path was available to me…! I haven't given up on getting a Dia skill. Once I get that, the first thing I'm gonna do is kill you and take revenge…!" Aiden bared his teeth in sinister hate. Lululee froze on the spot.

As she stood there, unable to say a word, she felt a tug on her arm—it was Lowe. "Let's go, Lululee. You're satisfied now, right?" he asked lazily, while picking his ear with his pinkie. But his pull on Lululee's arm was strong, as if he would not accept any alternatives.

"B-but—"

"You're not gonna reach him. Any more is just pouring oil on the flames," Lowe said, and then without so much as a good-bye, he dragged Lululee off.

"Get lost…! Get lost, you murderer!!"

That cry of hate and the sound of a fist striking the iron bars rang out endlessly through the dark underground prison.

27

"Mm! So this is beef imported from the Rosagne region?!"

Holding a piece of boned meat in her right hand and a tankard filled to the brim with booze in her left, Alina widened her eyes from the softness of the food she'd just sank her teeth into. She washed down that bite of her spiced and salty treat with a drink.

"Ahhhh! Heaven!"

Savoring the Centennial Festival booze that she'd finally gotten a taste of, Alina looked around the main street. The festival music was lively, delicious smells tickled her nose, and everyone was having fun. Even though it was the same road she usually took to work, it was as if she had come to a completely different world. Her annual frustration over not being able to attend, plus overcoming an unprecedented amount of overtime this year, made the event even more moving.

"I did it… I won this…! Freedom and dignity as a laborer…!!"

Only someone who had gone through overtime hell and back in order to attend the Centennial Festival would understand this feeling of release and joy.

Say what you will about the carrot and the stick, but people could not live on the stick alone. It was that carrot in the distance that enabled them to give their all every day. Having only ever gotten hit with the stick while missing out on the carrot, Alina was moved to tears.

"Today, I'm going to forget all about stupid work, and have *so* much fun…!"

Gobbling down the last of her meat, Alina looked around for her next target. Proud chefs had set out street stalls around the main road. Being able to enjoy cuisines from other nations on the continent that you normally would never taste was one of the attractions of the Centennial Festival. As Alina was trembling in determination, someone called out to her in surprise, their voice quivering.

"You eat quite a lot, huh, Alina?" It was Jade. "I eat what you'd expect for my physique, but you're so thin—where does all that food go?"

"Heh…"

With a munch and a gulp as she swallowed the meat in her, she licked the juices stuck around her mouth and then smiled boldly. "My digestive organs were trained with regular overdrinking and overeating to vent stress. You can't underestimate that."

"…So what are you going to have next?"

"Hmm, yeah. We've basically gone through all the stalls that will sell out—so next is the sweets!"

Pulling out her handmade guidebook to the Centennial Festival, Alina began looking for her next stop with utmost seriousness. "I hear they're selling a fun dessert in the big square. They're candy-coated fruit."

"Huh, that sounds good. The big event of the first day is about to start too, so this is just about perfect."

The Centennial Festival was held for three days and three nights, and there was a big event in the main square every day. Specially selected performers who had polished their skills for the occasion would put on a show, with a parade from a band of musicians. To top it all off, a completely different type of spectacle would close out the Centennial Festival on the final show of the third day.

"Then let's go, Alina."

As Alina was gleefully tucking her guidebook into the pouch at her waist, Jade held out his hand to her.

"...?" Alina didn't get what he meant for a moment and stared blankly at his palm.

Jade smirked back at her. "The square is more crowded than here. Let's hold hands so we don't get split up."

"I don't care if we get split up." Alina rejected him coldly.

But Jade seemed a little different from usual, as an intimidating aura seemed to be emanating from his right hand. "No, we can't have that...! I've...been waiting for this opportunity for so long...! You've had meat and booze and stuff in your hands this entire time...! But now they're finally free, and I won't let this chance get away from me...!"

"Oh-ho... What a selfish thing to say." Alina glared sharply at Jade, her green eyes flashing. "At festivals, you walk around with booze in one hand and food in the other! Having one occupied with anything else is out of the question! Besides, who the hell would hold hands with you, you creepy silver freak—?" Alina's war hammer just about popped out as she disparaged him like usual, but then she managed to catch herself.

"Hmm? What's wrong, Alina?"

After practically having said he was going to hold hands with her that day, even if it meant getting hit, Jade could only tilt his head. She had suddenly stopped disparaging him and started fidgeting instead. She was silent for a while before she started glaring alternately between Jade's face and the hand that he'd offered her.

"...I-it's not really...well, um," she stuttered.

Alina had suddenly given up trying to punch Jade...because she was thankful to him, more or less.

If not for his help with overtime, she never would have been able to come to the Centennial Festival like she'd wanted so badly. If not for him, Alina would have been tearfully doing overtime while listening to the festival music again this year. Nothing made her happier than the fact he'd averted this tragic future for her.

"No way—does your stomach hurt or something?!" Seeing Alina clearly different from usual, Jade forgot about holding her hand and started to freak out. "Or did you drink too much? You've really been tossing it back, after all…! Hold on, I'll get you some water."

When he turned away to search for water, Alina steeled herself and grabbed his hand.

"…Huh?" Jade made a bewildered noise as he was about to run off, then froze for a moment. He turned around with much trepidation.

Alina was holding his hand.

His jaw dropped. Alina looked away, cheeks slightly red as she muttered under her breath, "…Th-this is…well, if you hadn't helped me with overtime, then I definitely wouldn't have been able to come to the Centennial Festival this year… Um…ah, what I mean is…" For some reason, she couldn't quite be honest with him, but she recovered with a snort and said, "Um…thanks."

Jade's eyes went wide, and he stood there like a stone statue, opening and closing his mouth in a daze. He was stuck like that for a while, but the sensation of Alina's hand finally brought him back to his senses.

"Yeah!"

Smiling happily, he squeezed her small palm back.

28

"Shit! Those assholes, looking down on me…"

Aiden punched at the bars of his underground cell as hard as he could. Listening to the sound reverberate through the eerie

underground prison, he bared his teeth and glared down the hallway where that healer and her friend had gone.

"That...murderer!!"

Was this anger or hate? Unable to restrain his raging emotions, Aiden raised his shackled leg to kick aggressively at the bars, again and again. He didn't let up, even when the shackles dug into his flesh and drew blood.

"Haah, haah!"

After a while, Aiden finally stopped kicking, his shoulders heaving as he caught his breath. The stinging pain actually felt pleasant. He wanted to saturate his brain with pain to numb himself to reality. As he was thinking this, tears dribbled from his eyes.

"Ngh...hnn."

Smothering his voice, Aiden cried. As if being hit with the backlash of his emotional outburst, he was assaulted by his usual self-loathing.

He was the real murderer here.

Aiden knew that he was responsible for his party getting wiped out. Not only had he been unable to hold the enemy's aggro, but he'd also suggested challenging the boss in the first place. The other members of his party—Lululee in particular—had been strongly against it, but Aiden hadn't listened at all and had gone to face the boss anyway.

In the confusion, Lululee had continued to heal them until her magic powers had run out. Meanwhile, Aiden had wavered over whether to retreat after he found himself unable to pull their foe's aggro back on himself, letting his allies die without doing anything.

"No, it's not my fault...! It's all because of skills! It's because I can't manifest a skill...!"

He envied Lululee for having manifested a Sigurth skill. Vicious jealousy laid its roots in Aiden's heart and continued to eat away at it. The only way to get rid of that envy was to get stronger. He had to manifest a skill. And not some half-assed ability but an exceptional one.

Just then, a gentle voice rang out. "You're pretty unruly there."

Aiden raised his head with a start. He hadn't noticed that two men were standing on the other side of the bars.

It was Heitz, wearing his usual nonchalant smile. Another man loomed behind him in silence. He really was as quiet as people said; Aiden had never seen him speak once, nor had he heard anyone call him by any name. Could he not talk, or did he just not want to? Aiden didn't know a thing about him.

"...That skill of yours sure is amazing," said Aiden. "You can even get into the guild's underground prison?"

Heitz had a teleportation Sigurth skill. Fighting back his hatred for anyone who possessed a Sigurth skill, Aiden turned his head away.

"Not at all," said Heitz. "My skill isn't so amazing that I can warp to a single cell to infiltrate a complex and mazelike underground prison. I actually got permission and came in legitimately through the entrance."

Heitz gave him a dubious smile, then held up the book he had in hand to show him. "I had business at a level far below here. I just came to get a dear friend while I was at it."

"...What's this business of yours?"

"You don't know? It's a hidden quest. Though I have yet to accept it."

"!" Aiden widened his eyes. It seemed like just a book, but upon closer inspection, the binding was densely covered in conspicuous golden characters.

"I went to go borrow something that was carefully tucked away in the underground book storage."

"Underground book storage?!"

Aiden gawked at the unexpected phrase that spilled from Heinz's mouth. That was on the lowest level of the underground maze, and only the guildmaster was allowed to enter. It was said that the most confidential secrets of the Adventurers Guild were kept there.

"…No way. You're not going to tell me that the man in black is the person who set all this up for us, are you…?!"

"You've got it. I am thankful indeed for his infinitely generous contributions."

"Who the hell is he?!"

Aiden had only ever seen the man in black—the person who had told Heitz about the relic that could grant a Dia skill—once. He was clad in ebon robes like burial clothes that hid his face, so although they could tell from his low voice that he was a man, they didn't know who he really was. He had appeared to them out of the blue, only to vanish again once they'd finished talking.

Remembering that mysterious person made Aiden shiver and go pale.

Not only had they broken into the lowest level of the guild prison, they'd gotten Heitz into the underground books storage that only the guildmaster had the right to peruse—they were clearly not just anyone.

Heitz tilted his head slightly at Aiden's frozen expression. "Who knows? I'm not particularly interested, and I'm not going to go tactlessly prying. If I can get their help, I'll take it, no matter who they are."

"…"

Just like when Aiden had first met the man, Heitz was mild mannered at a glance, but when you really looked closely, his horrifying smile suggested a bottomless darkness.

"Don't you want to get back at this miserable world with us?"

So Heitz had sweetly whispered to Aiden back when he'd been despairing over his inability to manifest a skill. Heitz's invitation had seemed like a ray of light at the time, since Aiden had almost resigned himself to the fact that he would never obtain a skill. Now, however, he felt some belated unease, wondering if it was a good idea to associate with the man.

"Soon, Ricaide will cause a little bit of a commotion at the festival for us. We'll take advantage of that confusion to get up top," Heitz explained as he unlocked the cell with a key that he'd pulled out—he must have gotten in from the man in black. Ricaide was the black mage from their party. He was a man with a rail-thin body who always laughed in an annoying way, like he was mocking you.

"Come on, let's go. We've been beaten down for so long, but now our victory is right in front of us."

The bars of the door opened with an eerie creak. Heitz spread his hands as if welcoming Aiden. It was like Aiden was looking at the mouth of hell.

…What am I so freaked out about? There's nothing to feel anxious about, at this point.

He'd already made up his mind that he would do anything to manifest a skill. He was never going to get one from living an honest life. He had to accomplish this, even if he went off the straight and narrow.

"…Yeah. Let's go." Aiden forced himself to smile and took a step forward.

There was no turning back now.

29

Alina reached the main square to find the area a swirl of even greater enthusiasm.

The square was the center of the festival, and the hustle and bustle was particularly loud here since the area was packed. The perimeter of the square was surrounded by street stalls, with owners who had fought to get this prime location. Brilliant lights gushed from the stalls, and there were lines everywhere. The special stage that was to be unveiled on the third day was still covered with a cloth.

"Wow, there's sure a lot of excitement, huh?" Jade was giddy and pleased with himself, his cheeks flushed with joy. He'd been holding Alina's hand tight for a while now, and he hadn't let go for a single instant. "I never thought the day would come when I could hold hands with you... I'm so glad I didn't give up on it."

"...H-holding hands isn't a good thing at all. It's inconvenient to have one hand occupied." Alina scowled to hide her embarrassment.

Jade smiled wryly. "Alina, a girl of your age should be more like, well, you know..."

Ignoring his babbling, she pointed at the street stall she was after. Seeing there was already a long line, she dashed off without a thought. "Ah, there it is! Over there, over there! We have to go right now, or they'll sell ou—"

But Alina stopped halfway—because the performance of a black mage entertainer showing off their magical craft in the corner of the square caught her eye.

Standing in the center of a little cluster of people, the entertainer wore a colorful mask, shooting water in midair and turning it into shapes of animals and monsters, freezing it into beautiful shells of ice to excite the audience. It was an old-fashioned art that stuck close to tradition, but the audience was completely absorbed, caught up in the festive atmosphere.

It was an unremarkable sight decorating a corner of the festival, but a strange, indescribable premonition drew Alina's gaze toward it.

Jade allowed her to draw him along but was perplexed when she stopped abruptly. "What is it, Alina?" he asked her. He saw that her gaze was fixed on a single spot, and he followed it to look at the entertainer.

Once the man was done his set of water tricks, he waved his finger with a "Tsk-tsk-tsk," as if to say, *This is only the beginning.* With the audience's expectations swelling, he held his hand up and said a single word:

"Glassis."

It came so fast that nobody was able to tell that was an attack spell. With a hard cracking noise, the incantation froze a cluster of people in the front row.

"...Huh?"

A man who'd happened to escape danger stared blankly at the audience member frozen beside him. During that time, the entertainer raised both hands high into the sky and yelled, "Imber!"

Instantaneously, countless chunks of ice shot into the sky. When they reached their apex, the chunks reflected the lights of the festival, growing faster and larger, then rained down on the ground. The projectiles struck the ground with a crash, freezing people and stalls on impact.

"Wha...magic?!"

"This is no performance! This is—black magic!"

A shriek went up somewhere. That was the beginning, and as the other members of the audience recognized the danger, they all surged toward the square exit at once, trying to get as far from the entertainer as possible. Screams and yells flew everywhere, and everything was plunged into chaos.

"Don't let go of my hand, Alina!"

Alina was so petite, she was just about instantly swallowed up by the rampaging waves of people, but Jade somehow held his ground and kept a firm hold on her hand. The entertainer was cackling eerily at the confusion around him, but he wasn't attacking the people any further, just gleefully watching the confusion.

Eventually, Alina and Jade made it through the raging waves of people, and once things finally calmed down and they could move around again, Jade immediately drew the sword at his belt that he carried for self-defense and faced off against the entertainer. Behind Jade, Alina looked around in shock at the complete transformation of the square.

"The...the Centennial Festival..."

The street stalls that had enlivened the main festival venue until just a few seconds ago were crushed, delicious-looking foods had fallen to be trampled underfoot, and the decorations that were set up a few days ago had been ripped apart and frozen. Not even a trace of the carefree festival atmosphere remained.

"The Cen…Cen…Centennial…"

She'd been looking forward to the Centennial Festival all this time; she couldn't accept that it was destroyed. Her mind went white.

How could anyone be so cruel?

Alina had worked day in and day out to attend the Centennial Festival. She had withstood the rush of adventurers from that cold-hearted rumor, and she'd overcome an unprecedented amount of overtime through her wholehearted vow to experience the festival this year. When times had been tough, just thinking about the Centennial Festival had made strength well up inside her.

It wasn't just a fun event to her. It was not simply a reward. It was a ceremony for taking back her life after pushing through day after day of drudgery—this was about reaffirming her freedom and dignity.

And now that was lost. Because of this incomprehensibly sudden attack from this incomprehensible entertainer.

"……………………………………Unforgivable………………
…," Alina muttered softly. Her gaze was on the entertainer who stood eerily in the main square. He was looking at Alina like a predator eyeing its prey.

The entertainer swung his rod. Instantly, the magic sigil of an attack spell appeared underneath Alina's feet. Pillars of ice rose up and knocked Jade away from her, imprisoning Alina in a giant cage of ice.

"A-Alina!"

"Jaaade Scraaade from Siiilver Swooord," the entertainer said in a strange, put-on voice as he looked at Jade. "Thiiis girl is my hostage."

"Your hostage?!"

Jade panicked, thinking, *Alina, of all people?*

The entertainer snorted at him. "Iiif you feeear for heeer liiife, then bring the Exeeecuuutioner."

"The Executioner…?! U-uh, I think you're probably the one who should be fearing for your—"

"Skill Activate: *Dia Break!*" Cutting off Jade's babbling, Alina activated her skill inside the small cage of ice.

Her war hammer appeared in a white glow that tore through the night. Weapon in hand, Alina shattered the ice cage with a *snap*. Shards of ice burst into bits that flew in all directions, sweeping up dust that covered her field of view.

"Ahh! Hold on, hold on!" Jade cried out in panic as something came fluttering toward her.

It was a cheap cloak that had been dropped in the square in the midst of the confusion. Alina donned the outfit he'd hastily tossed to her without a word.

The entertainer seemed a bit confused, and when he saw who appeared from behind the curtain of ice—Alina, with the hood of the cloak completely covering her face, gripping a silver war hammer in her right hand—he called out in even greater surprise. "E-Exeeecuuutioner…?! Just wheeere did you co— *Blerk!*"

She didn't even let the entertainer get halfway before she slammed the shocked man with her war hammer.

"Agh, urgh, buh!" He cried out like any other person as he lightly rolled over the flagstones.

Alina was deliberately holding back her strength. Not because she didn't want to kill him, but because there was no way she was going to let him off with a single wallop when he'd gotten up to such evil deeds.

"W…wait…liiisten to my go—" This piddling entertainer, still trying to maintain his weird way of talking even as he staggered to his feet, reached out to try to pick his rod up off the ground.

But Alina was there instantly, stomping hard on his arm.

"Ow, ow, ow, ow!"

"I don't care about your goals. More importantly, do you understand *what* you've done? Do you know what the Centennial Festival represented to me...?"

Behind her, Jade trembled as he sheathed his sword, muttering, "My condolences."

"I've been looking forward to this night for *sooooooo* long... I've been working overtime for days now and *finally* got to relax...!"

Alina set down her war hammer. Ignoring how the impact dented the ground, she cracked her knuckles with her freed hands.

"Wh-what...?"

"Don't think you're going to get an easy death."

Her eyes were wide and blazing, while her lips were the opposite, drawn up in a smile. The entertainer must have noticed the intensity of her murderous aura, as he had finally frozen up.

Alina grabbed him by the lapels, made a fist, and then suddenly put on a low voice as she said, "You...asshole entertainer...!!"

Alina slammed her fist into his face. He went flying with a "*Hrk!*" and Alina followed, straddling him to punch him again and again. The entertainer completely gave up on talking in that creepy way, and his screams echoed over and over through the square. It took quite a while before the beating was over.

30

Lululee's shoulders drooped sadly as Lowe took her by the hand, silently walking through the underground prison.

Having finished that miserable reunion with Aiden, they used the red crystal gate to return to where the underground prison watchman was. Lowe was practically dragging her out by force, but it was clear there was no point in Lululee and Aiden seeing any more of each other. Besides, it didn't feel good to watch his friend getting verbally abused, either.

"Let's go, Lululee. We can go to the festival tomorrow."

"…Okay," she replied, her voice small and weak. That was little wonder, considering her personality. Lowe had expected things would turn out like this, but he was still incredibly aggravated as he cursed Aiden in his head.

Seriously, what is his deal…? He's just taking everything out on her… Maybe I'll gouge out his other eye…

Right as he was vaguely entertaining such violent thoughts, it happened.

A low shudder ran through the underground prison.

"Yeek…!"

Lululee immediately staggered, and Lowe caught her, brow furrowing. The shaking only lasted an instant before it quickly settled, loosening a bit of dust from the labyrinth's ancient ceiling.

"What was that rumbling? Was that from town…?" asked Lowe. "Did something happen at the festival?"

"Let's—" Lowe was about to say *let's go* when suddenly, a chill ran down his spine.

"Lowe?"

Seeing that the black mage had come to a sudden stop, Lululee tilted her head. Lowe was paralyzed, unable to reply. That was because he'd heard a low humming sound behind him. The red crystal gate made that sound when it was operating.

His heart thudded. As Lululee shot Lowe a questioning look, he placed her behind his back and slowly turned around.

A man appeared from the red crystal gate. He was a middle-aged adventurer with a mild-mannered air who looked like he wouldn't hurt a fly—that familiar face belonged to Heitz, the person who had been spreading the rumor around the Forest of Eternity.

"Oh?" Heitz's gaze met with Lowe's, but he wasn't rattled at all, twisting his face in mock surprise. "You caught me in a bad moment."

"Why...are you...here...?!" Lowe's voice was hoarse.

This was a different situation from their encounter in the Forest of Eternity. You needed to get permission to enter the underground prison. Even an ordinary adventurer shouldn't have been able to get in here, never mind adventurers who should have been stripped of their licenses for their malicious deeds.

"Watchman! Why did you let him through?!" Lowe yelled at the jailer of the underground prison, who stood there to the side like a machine even now. "Didn't these guys have their licenses stripped?"

"They had permission. We don't check for whether visitors are licensed or not," was all the watchman said robotically.

"You're telling me you let them through...?!"

Confused, Lowe gazed at the two men who appeared from behind Heitz. There was a silent adventurer with his lips drawn in a thin line and a man with one eye and one arm. It was Aiden, who had been in one of the underground cells until a moment ago.

"A-Aiden...?!" Lululee cried out quietly in shock.

"You've got permission to take a prisoner out of here, too...?!" said Lowe.

"I was directed to release him," said the jailer.

"There's no way!" Lowe cried. "Did you really check?! There's no way the guild would ever give that—"

"You are not in the position to know the answer to that question. I only follow orders and let people with permission through."

"...!"

"That's how it is, Mr. Silver Sword. But shouldn't you be worrying more about this?"

Heitz was holding an old tome, but it wasn't just any book. It was packed with golden characters that didn't match the binding, and it emitted a pale glow in the dark of the underground prison.

Lowe widened his eyes, and his breath caught. "A secret... quest...?!"

He had heard from Jade that secret quests were written in golden letters.

"We went to go borrow this from the guild's underground book storage. Aw, they should have just told us that they'd found this. It's so unfair of them to quietly hide it away in the depths of the earth."

Not giving them the time to stop him, Heitz casually opened the book.

"Sto—"

There was a dazzling flash, and the golden characters flew into the air.

DESIGNATED ADVENTURER RANK: N/A

LOCATION: THE FOREST OF ETERNITY

ACHIEVEMENT CONDITIONS: DEFEAT ALL FLOOR BOSSES

REQUEST GIVER WILL NOT BE INDICATED. RECEIVER SIGNATURE ABRIDGED.

RECEIPT OF QUEST ACKNOWLEDGED AS PER ABOVE.

The Forest of Eternity...?!

The familiar terms for receiving a quest were in gold. Lowe furrowed his brow at the quest.

The characters soundlessly faded into thin air. But it was certain that the gold characters unfurling in the air had said, "The Forest of Eternity"—the C-rank dungeon where many beginning adventurers would first camp out.

But now the quest had been taken. The hidden dungeon had appeared.

"You...!" Grinding his teeth, Lowe glared at Heitz. "Do you really believe you can get your hands on a Dia skill?!"

"It's because we do that we've come this far—no, that's not quite right. To be more precise, the relic isn't one that can get you a Dia skill, but a special relic that *contains* Dia skills, known as a 'dark god.'"

H-he knows about the dark gods...?!

"Well, if we mentioned *dark gods*, then nobody would search for secret quests for us, so we dramatized things a bit. Perhaps we went a bit too far with it? The adventurers went out of control for a while there. Well, they did find us a secret quest in the end, so I suppose even the incompetent can pull it off, with a little coaxing."

The thin smile on Heitz's face contrasted sharply with Lowe's consternation. Even though the man knew about the dark gods, he must not have been aware of the seriousness of what he'd just done, as he was shrugging nonchalantly.

"Now then, since I went to the trouble of taking the quest right in front of you, I take it that Silver Sword will be coming? To the hidden dungeon."

"...What do you mean?"

"I'm inviting all of you. How about we see the dark god together? I'll leave it up to you whether to come or not. Skill Activate: *Sigurth Mover.*"

Heitz activated his skill, and then he vanished beyond the red glow. Lowe hastily drew his rod.

"Wait! If you revive a dark god—"

But before he could activate his magic, the light faded, and Heitz and his party vanished.

****

Alina sat on a bench in the square in a daze. The entertainer's attack had left the place almost empty, and Alina stared into space like a ghost. When she lifted her chin slightly, it seemed like her soul would slip out from her half-open mouth.

"Festival...canceled... Festival...canceled..."

She repeated those words of despair with vacant eyes. A few

stragglers still wandered the grounds in confusion, though most of the visitors had departed. The only people who remained were drunks who couldn't figure out what was going on and adventurers with nerves of steel. With this kind of uproar, there was no way the festival wouldn't be canceled.

Guild security had come rushing in at some point, and out of the corner of her eye, Alina saw Jade handing the entertainer over to them. The entertainer's face was crushed now. Though they'd taken off his mask, his face was so swollen from the beating he'd taken that he was no longer identifiable. Apparently, they were going to question him after he'd been healed. Alina would have liked to tear the man apart about a hundred million more times, but Jade had stopped her.

"Alina, are you alive?" Jade asked awkwardly when he returned.

With her dead brain, Alina muttered back, "...I'm dead..."

"They're saying that they're going to restart the festival in a bit."

"Really?!" Alina squeaked, clinging to Jade.

"Since it was just the square that got attacked, and we caught the culprit... Still, I'm sure it wouldn't hurt to cancel things... But that's Iffole for you. A little danger isn't going to stop them from continuing the festivities."

"Wh-what a reliiiiiief!" Alina's whole body went slack, and she slumped to the ground at Jade's feet.

"This is the one day...I'm thankful that Iffole...is a city of gutsy adventurers..."

A few seconds later and she was back on her feet again, thrusting her right fist up high with her eyes sparkling. "Now that it's settled, this isn't the time to be dawdling around here! Let's go to lots of the places we haven't—"

"Leader!"

Right as Alina had gotten all her energy back, a pale-looking adventurer ran up to them.

It was Lowe. And behind him was Lululee, too. For some reason, the two of them were fully equipped for a dungeon, and Lowe had his rod in hand.

"Hey, you two. Why are you dressed like that?" Jade asked.

"A secret quest got issued!!"

Both Alina and Jade blinked at his sudden declaration.

"Huh?"

"What?" They were both bewildered.

Lowe, looking like he was at the end of his rope, wiped at the sweat on his neck as he rattled off to them, "It's Heitz! He stole a secret quest that the guild had found and accepted it! The hidden dungeon is supposed to be in the Forest of Eternity... They're planning on resurrecting a dark go—"

"I'll get armored up! I'll hear the rest on the way!" Jade cut Lowe off, immediately grasping the situation and pulling out his adventurer license card. Next, he turned to Alina.

"You come with...!" But then Jade suddenly stopped halfway. "Wait, no. Don't come."

"...Huh? But..."

"You've been working hard all this time for the festival, right?"

Jade clapped a hand on Alina's head, and he didn't look at her again. Instead, he fixed his sharp gaze on Lowe and Lululee, telling them in a serious tone, "We're going to stop Heitz before he resurrects a dark god. They've already been stripped of their adventurers' licenses, so they shouldn't be able to use the crystal gates. If they're heading to the Forest of Eternity on foot, then we still have time.

"Huh? Hey, hold on."

Jade briskly gave the order, then strode toward the crystal gate in the square. Left behind, Alina tried to hurry after him, but then she turned back around.

Her eyes fell on the lights of the festival, which was on the verge of reopening. Alina had the right to enjoy it. She'd been working so hard for it—since months back. No, since before that. She'd been crushed by overtime during the Centennial Festival the past two years, so she'd vowed to attend it this year.

But as Alina watched Silver Sword go, an uneasy feeling stirred in her heart. If they could prevent the resurrection of a dark god, then things would be fine. But what if the worst happened? What if they never came back?

"We'll take the crystal gate to guild headquarters, get equipped, and head out right away. If a dark god gets revived as we feared—" Jade stopped halfway through that remark. Alina grabbed his sleeve with her fingers, holding him back.

"I'm going, too."

She wasn't dragging her feet like she had a month ago. She knew now what was most important to her.

"...Alina..." Jade turned around to find Alina, a conflicted expression on her face.

Looking right back at him with strength in her jade-green eyes, Alina said, "I don't want you guys to die."

Jade's face twisted in frustration for a moment, but he must have seen even that hesitation as a hindrance in their battle against time, because he looked away and muttered, "Thanks. I'm sorry, Alina..."

31

Jade got himself equipped at the guild headquarters, then headed to the Forest of Eternity with everyone in a few minutes.

As soon as they entered the forest, Jade unleashed his skill. "Skill Activate: *Sigurth Beast*!"

Sigurth Beast made Jade's senses—like sight, hearing and smell—sharper than those of humans, enabling him to search for enemies over a wide area.

A vast swath of information instantly surged to him—from the

smell of the wind making the trees sway to the sound of tiny creatures' footsteps racing over branches. And in that noise, Jade noticed
something strange.

"Mossy Rock Lake..."

That landmark was often used as a resting place because its low
ether density kept monsters away. But now there was ether there,
and it was thick, condensed to a repulsive degree.

"Something's strange. Let's go."

Now that Lowe had gotten him caught up on everything, Jade
ran for Mossy Rock Lake as he considered once again how abnormal this situation was.

*Heitz got permission to go into the underground prison, let Aiden
escape, and even stole a tome containing a hidden quest from the underground book storage... Is that even possible?*

The subterranean maze the guild had turned into a prison had
another use.

They'd converted floor thirty-three, the lowest level of the labyrinth, into a storehouse for valuable books. It held both tomes that
were too sensitive to release to the public and dangerous relics.
Only the guildmaster was allowed in. If you were going to store a
secret quest, that would be the place.

However, the underground book storage was not managed by the
jailer. It should have been impossible for outsiders to get in there.

But what if...?

Jade suddenly hit upon an unpleasant possibility.

A dark-skinned man crossed his mind.

Those deep-set eyes and that dignified face carved with wrinkles. That physique no lesser than that of a young person. A cape
emblazoned with the guild crest fluttering behind the man, whose
amiable personality clashed with his rugged looks and who was
said to be the strongest of adventurers in his youth.

*Could Glen have told Heitz about it...? No...no way...it couldn't
be... I'm overthinking things.*

That was way too wild an idea. Glen would have no reason to do something so foolish.

Which means this must be the work of the man in black...

The person who'd told Rufus and Heitz about the dark gods; he was the one pulling the strings behind the scenes, making people look for hidden quests and trying to get them to unseal the deities. Considering he'd let people into the underground prison and freed one of its inmates, he had to be far from ordinary.

The man in black... Who is he...?!

And now, a crisis had erupted from what should have been mere rumors. Jade's blood ran cold as he considered the unfathomable nature of the man behind it all. But he drove those doubts into the back of his mind for the moment. For now, he had to tackle the issue that was right in front of them.

When they arrived at Mossy Rock Lake, it was evident that something had changed.

"This is..."

A hole had formed in the mossy rock, revealing a staircase descending underground. It went without saying, but those hadn't been there when they'd come a few days ago.

"Glassis." Lowe froze the lake, making a path to the rock.

Stopping for a moment in front of the stairs, Jade cautiously investigated the hole and the stairs within. It was too dark to see inside, and the presence of ether far thicker than that wafting in the forest was leaking out.

"Even with *Sigurth Beast*, I can't see down the stairs... It looks like it leads pretty far down. And the ether's dense, too... There's definitely a boss room ahead."

"Underground...? But the Forest of Eternity only has a single level—are you telling me there's another?" Alina asked.

Jade nodded. "...A hidden floor...no, maybe this underground area is the *real* dungeon here. It's possible that the ether in the Forest of Eternity leaked out of the hidden dungeon."

"Let's go," he said, starting to head down the stairs. Something like the light of a skill glowed on the wall of the long stairway, shining in geometric patterns. Lowe produced an orb of light to make things easier to see, but even without his magic, it was only bright enough that you could clearly make out the ground. Eventually, they came to see the end of the stairs, where they stopped at...

"Is this...a boss room...?"

The presence of ether was thick. A set of wide-open iron doors stood before them, leading to a mysterious cave.

It was a calm, chilly space, large enough to rival the guild headquarters' training grounds. The walls were bare stone and glowed a pale blue. Water was dripping down from the high domed roof, and there were a number of puddles on the floor, plus a large magic sigil emitting a pale gleam.

"My, it seems you got ahead of us," came a voice from behind them. They turned around to find Heitz's party coming down the stairs.

Though it was hard to believe that Aiden really had escaped from the underground prison, Jade finally had to face facts when he saw the man following along nonchalantly.

"I see you went to the trouble of calling the Executioner as well. How wonderful." Heitz shifted his gaze to Alina, clad in the Executioner's cloak. "Well, I suppose that's no surprise. If a dark god is revived, even Silver Sword wouldn't go un—"

"Imber!" Lowe chanted a spell, interrupting Heitz's snide remarks. Forget introductions—they couldn't let Heitz and his party do as they pleased any longer.

Lowe had chanted the same ice spell that the entertainer had used, but his version was no mere hailstorm. The countless frozen chunks that manifested in the air obeyed Lowe's will like a school of fish, striking the limbs of everyone in Heitz's party. It took a lot of skill to direct Imber's ice chunks at specific targets.

"Watch out...!"

The opposing group all watched as their arms and legs froze before their eyes, but Aiden was the only one to panic. By contrast, Heitz and the man in black didn't struggle at all, just looked down in silence as they froze over.

"Oh-ho. I've never seen such fine control of area of attack magic. Your black mage has certainly earned his place in Silver Sword. Wonderful."

"I'm not about to let you revive a dark god…!" cried Lowe.

"Oh, really? But you can't dispose of us here, since the resurrection of a god requires the souls of humans. However, there's nothing stopping us from killing all of you."

"Ah… So then you think you have the advantage? You guys can just sit there and freeze!"

"Skill Activate."

But right before they could be completely encased in ice, the silent man who had been in waiting behind Heitz sluggishly opened his mouth for the first time.

"*Sigurth Offer.*"

The effect was instantaneous.

The red light of a Sigurth skill shined from the man. There came a *squelch*, and then his body burst open from the inside, ice from the Imber spell and all. A sticky red substance splattered over the entire cave, lumps of flesh flying in a gooey mess.

"…?!" Jade froze in shock.

Behind him, Lululee let out a small scream.

At the same time, the thick ice that had covered Heitz's party audibly crumbled.

"Ohh, that was a pretty dramatic death." Having escaped from his bindings, Heitz dispassionately examined the lumps of his comrade's flesh that were sitting in a puddle of blood. "Apparently, his skill nullifies any and all attacks on his allies in exchange for his life. Perhaps it was a waste to use it just for undoing some black magic, though."

"...He...blew himself up...?" Lowe blanched, looking on in shock at the puddle of blood that continued to spread.

Like Jade's *Sigurth Blood*, *Sigurth Offer* was a skill that could reap incredible results, provided that the user damaged themself. In the silent man's case, he would have been able to cancel out a variety of powerful abilities by giving up his life.

But Heitz didn't care about that. His only objective had been getting his follower to kill himself.

In order to revive the dark god.

"Wasn't that a wonderful display of self-sacrifice? I can't help but feel sympathy that he manifested such a worthless skill." The only sound in the silence of the cave was Heitz's chuckling.

"...C...come on... What the hell...?" Aiden muttered, voice trembling. Jade wasn't the only one paling at the gruesome sight. Aiden's eyes were wide as he pressed Heitz. "D...did he...blow himself up...?!"

"It's just as you see. And is there something wrong with that, Aiden?" Heitz gave the pallid adventurer a gentle look. No—though his gaze appeared gentle, it was quietly insane. "I explained before, didn't I? The resurrection of a dark god requires a human soul. Don't you think this is the most effective use of his skill?"

"You...you never...told me about this...! What the hell?!" Aiden backed away, his face ashen. "You said that the dark gods who slumber in hidden dungeons will grant you a Dia skill..."

"Oh dear, did you actually believe that something so convenient existed?" Heitz blinked incredulously.

"Wha...wha...?"

"It's all right, I made sure to have a job for you, too. We are offerings to the great dark god. We have gathered in order to be devoured by this superior being, that it might gain even greater powers. I actually wanted to bring Ricaide—the man who caused that incident in the festival—here as well, but it seems that he got arrested."

"Why are you going so far to try to revive this dark god?!" Jade yelled, unable to take it. "What point is there in all this…?! You'll just get yourself killed!"

"…Why, you ask? Well, I'm sure you wouldn't get it. Someone from Silver Sword who accomplishes spectacular feats every day with their amazing skills wouldn't understand the lowest class of adventurer, suffering at the bottom with trash-tier abilities…"

Heitz sighed, then continued, "My skill, *Sigurth Mover*, seems convenient, but it has a fatal restriction: I can't choose where it sends me. It's basically only good for fleeing." The look in Heitz's eyes was gentle yet drenched in a keen hate. "Of course, this was valuable when I was starting out. But once my allies leveled up and no longer needed an emergency escape route, they quickly got rid of me, laughing all the while as they called me a 'walking crystal gate.'"

"…!"

"Ha-ha…ha-ha-ha-ha-ha! It's funny, isn't it? A walking crystal gate! What a perfect nickname. Why do things like skills exist in this world anyway? You can't choose them yourself, and you can't learn or train with them like magic. It's pure luck whether you get one or not. If you're fortunate you'll have a great life, but if luck isn't on your side you'll have no choice but to crawl in the trash… Why in the world are things like this?" While swaying on his feet, Heitz widened his eyes and bared his teeth in a repulsive smile. "When I was feeling desperate, a man in black appeared and told me something. He said there were dark gods, divine beings that dwell on this earth—and that they can take this garbage world and return it to nothingness…!"

"The man in black—"

"He arranged everything for us. Things have gone so smoothly, thanks to him. I figured if I lured out Silver Sword, then the Executioner would come, too—and my hunch was correct. If I can even finish off the Executioner, then nobody will be able to thwart the dark god's rampage of destruction…! For the first time ever, the gods will be on my side! That's why—"

Heitz's speech was interrupted by a dull *squelch*.

A beat later, their noses caught the thick stench of blood.

"Huh...?" Amid the silence, a bewildered sound escaped Heitz's lips.

A cute little hand had erupted out of his chest, right where his heart was. Someone had ran their bare hand through his armor from behind.

The abnormal sight struck everyone there speechless.

In the silent cavern, Heitz stared down at the hand for a moment in shock. It was an incoherent way of going out, to die so suddenly to a superhuman power, but Heitz was wearing a smile of madness.

"The dark god...!!"

The cute hand withdrew from his back with a *slorp*, and Heitz crumpled to the ground. A fountain of blood erupted from his body, dyeing the area around him dark. But even though the man was on death's door, his eyes sparkled with insanity. He frantically turned around so that he could burn the sight of the dark god he adored into his eyes...

...Only for a little foot to stomp into his face.

"What a gross old man!"

Came that blunt remark, along with the giggling of a girl.

A young girl with long golden hair had emerged from the darkness to stamp on Heitz without warning.

But anyone could tell that she was no ordinary girl—buried at the base of her porcelain-white throat was a little stone that glowed an eerie black. She was wearing a cute frilly skirt like that of a doll's, but a cruel shadow played across her face as she looked down at Heitz like an insect.

Then she raised the corners of her lips, licked the blood on her hand, and kicked Heitz in the face. With a painful-sounding *crack*,

Heitz's neck snapped in the wrong direction, and his head went flying, scattering blood.

"…!"

The girl's petite leg was far too strong for its size. There was also a mark on her right cheek, where a smirk was pasted. It was a seal that looked like half of a sigil. Upon closer inspection, however, it was of a familiar shape.

It was half of the magic sigil patterned after a sun, which the ancients always carved into relics—the mark of Dia.

This was what the "special relics" adventurers had been telling tales about for so long really were: Living relics created from the ancients' lust for power. An evil memento that had ironically ended up wiping the ancients from the face of the earth.

A dark god.

"Viena…there are so many humans!"

One more little voice rang out from the icy cave.

Another girl popped her face out from behind the dark god with long golden hair. Just like the girl who was called Viena, she had a little dark god core buried at the base of her neck. No—the two had more than just that in common. Just like identical twins, they shared the same face, the same height, and the same color hair—even the half mark of Dia carved into their cheeks. They were differentiated only by the length of their hair, as the girl who'd appeared from behind had an even bob that stopped at her shoulders.

Jade stiffened at the twin girls before them. "There are…two dark gods?!"

Heedless of his concern, the little dark god with the long hair called Viena smiled. "Yeah, there are a bunch of humans, Fiena. They're our offerings." Viena's lips kept moving as she thrust her chubby, childlike hand out in front of her. "Chant: *Dia Morte.*"

Just then, the white light of a skill ran through the dark god core at Viena's throat. At the same instant, another white light raced

around her, etching a circle in the form of a giant magic sigil. Particles of light converged around her tiny hand, and a giant weapon appeared from thin air.

It was a great silver bow about twice her height.

Just like Alina, who could summon a war hammer, and the dark god Silha, who could produce a giant spear, Viena had called forth a giant, silver-ornamented weapon of her own. The god core at the base of her throat was blazing with the light of her skill.

"…!" Jade immediately turned his greatshield toward her and readied himself for battle.

But Viena didn't make to attack right away. Instead, she poked at her partner, Fiena, who was still hidden behind her. "You hurry up, too, Fiena."

"Fiena is doing it, too…?"

"Yep."

The short-haired girl timidly came forward like Viena, but in contrast with her twin's confidence, she muttered to activate her skill. "Chant…*Dia Morte.*"

Responding to her intonation, a silver great bow just like Viena's appeared from thin air. The two dark gods had activated the same skill like it was nothing.

Jade's breath caught. "Th-they share…a skill?!"

It was common knowledge among adventurers that skills were fundamentally individual talents and that no two were completely alike. What they had just witnessed was clearly out of the ordinary.

"Of course—since we're two as one." Viena snorted at Jade's shock, proudly puffing out her chest as she licked her lips like a hungry beast and eyed everyone there. "Aaaall right, which offering should we eat first?"

32

"Here they come, Lululee!" Jade called.

That snapped the white mage out of her stupor, and she hastily activated her skill. "Skill Activate: *Sigurth Revive!*"

This was Lululee's powerful Sigurth skill, which conferred potent automatic healing effects. She granted it to Jade, their tank, while also sincerely apologizing to Alina, "I'm sorry, Alina...! A Sigurth skill won't work on someone who possesses a Dia skill..."

"Unlike Jade, I'm not in the habit of getting beaten to a pulp, so I'll be fine. More importantly, you should get back, Lululee."

It wasn't like an apology from Lululee would do Alina any good, but it was in her nature as a healer to give one anyway. For a moment, she fell silent and grew very downcast before she hid herself behind some rocks, as instructed.

"Dammit, two dark gods...?!" Jade raised his greatshield and drew the longsword at his waist. Beside him, Alina eyed the enemy warily. She was on the verge of activating her skill, when...

"H-hmm?! Huh, a cutie? It's a cute boy! I found a cute boy!!" Viena's eyes suddenly sparkled. She'd turned her enthusiastic gaze on Jade, noticing his youthful features. Her innocent excitement was like a child's—but then she shattered that illusion by artlessly calling forth a silver arrow from her hand and nocking it in her bow at Jade. "One cutie boy soul for me!"

At the same time, Alina dashed out from beside Jade. "Skill Activate: *Dia Break!*"

Clasping the war hammer that had appeared with her intonation, Alina smacked Viena's arrow aside the moment it left the girl's bow. The arrow went in the other direction, snapped, and quickly dispersed into thin air.

Our powers aren't even...?!

The arrow had felt so light that Alina widened her eyes. When she'd crossed weapons with the dark god Silha, their strength had been so close that she struggled to overcome him. Was this just because of how a bow and arrow worked, or was there more to it than that...?

As Alina thought this over, she fixed her aim on Viena and dashed in. Viena met her attack, not in the least bit rattled to see that her first move had been easily struck aside. Despite Alina coming closer and closer, the dark god made no effort to evade. Not only that—she made no effort to defend herself either. Instead, she lackadaisically watched the war hammer.

Right before Alina struck, Fiena cut between them.

"?!"

The striking end of Alina's war hammer hit Fiena. Her blow blew away the entirety of the girl's upper body, the little god core in her throat and all.

She's soft...?!

The dark god Silha had possessed a sturdy body that repelled from Alina's Dia skill, her war hammer. Compared to that, Fiena's form was far more fragile than a human's—like paper. She'd felt so flimsy that a shudder ran down Alina's spine.

And that sensation proved correct.

"Wha...?!"

The half of Fiena's body that had been dramatically smashed off wriggled, and the dark god reformed in the blink of an eye. In less than a few seconds, Fiena had reconstituted herself, her clothes intact.

She had already drawn back her bow again, training her arrowhead at the spot between Alina's eyes.

"Ngh!" Alina wrenched herself aside just as a giant arrow skimmed past her ear.

Alina lost her balance slightly, and Viena aimed another arrow at her. "Hmm? Checkmate already?" she said with a smirk, then fired her arrow.

The attack caught Alina completely off guard—but it failed to hit its target, passing through empty air in vain.

"Huh? Where—"

She was above.

Having made an aggressive leap to evade the arrow, Alina looked down to find Viena glancing around in confusion.

"Haaaaaahhhh!" With a scream, Alina struck the top of Viena's head with the full force of her fall.

A dull *plunk* rang out in the pale blue of the cave. But yet again, her blow felt too light, without enough resistance.

Alina landed before Viena, who was standing there in a daze, her head and right shoulder torn off. There was no question that she'd destroyed the god core in Viena's throat. But…

"!"

Alina gasped. Viena's body wriggled around as it regenerated before her eyes, just like Fiena's had. Within seconds, the dark god was as good as new, core and all. She looked entirely unperturbed.

"…No way…do these guys have regenerative powers?!" Jade cried, finally figuring it out.

"Ding-ding," Viena acknowledged as she cackled. "I told you— we're two as one."

She stuck up her index finger in an adorable pose, her expression calm and collected. She was just like a child enjoying a game that she knew she would win.

"…It looks like they're a pair," Lowe muttered to Alina, who had retreated to Jade's side for the moment.

"What do you mean?"

"Well…there are some really annoying monsters out there that regenerate continuously. They keep proliferating forever until you hit their core."

"Yeah…they're trouble…" Nodding at Lowe's explanation, Jade continued. "And if those regenerating monsters come in pairs, two things can happen: Either they'll keep regrowing until you take out whichever monster is the 'main' body, or they'll keep proliferating as long as one of them remains… I bet this dark god is the latter type."

"The latter...?" asked Alina. "Huh, so you're saying they won't go down no matter how much I hit them?"

"There are things you can do against monsters like that—like softening them up equally, then finishing them off with a sweep from wide-area magic. But there isn't any area of effect magic that works against dark gods..." Lowe groaned uneasily.

"Our only option is to destroy both their god cores at once," Jade proposed, but his expression was grim. No wonder.

Alina also scowled, then muttered, "Uh, but attacking both at once with a war hammer... That's impossible..."

It would be one thing if she had a greatsword with a wide area of attack or black magic at her disposal—but war hammers fundamentally struck one thing at a time, so it was practically impossible to hit two targets at once with them, especially when those targets were bouncing around.

"..." Jade must also have understood it was an unreasonable demand. He fell silent as he warily observed the twin dark gods, desperately trying to think of a way to eke out a win.

"Agh, but what is this place anyway? It's so dark and dank and dreary!" Ignoring Alina and the others, Viena looked around the cave and breathed a big sigh. "And, like, it's totally lame that we only have one ability each. Bow and arrows are so boring and bland, it's hilarious. I'm sick of this thing! Don't you think so, too, Fiena?"

"...Fiena likes it a lot," the other girl insisted.

But Viena ignored her, hands on her cheeks in ecstasy. "For your sake, we've got to eat *lots* more offerings and get more abilities! I wonder if there'll be more offerings up above if we can get out of this wretched place?"

Viena gave a wicked smile that contrasted sharply with her adorable appearance, charging the air of the cave with tension.

On their way to the hidden dungeon, Jade had told Alina of his theory—that there were multiple Dia skills sealed in a god core and that a dark god could use as many Dia skills as the number of people they had slain. Inferring from what Viena had said, that theory was most likely correct.

The town closest to the Forest of Eternity was Iffole. Lots of people had gathered there today for the Centennial Festival. If Alina and the others all lost their lives, and the dark gods went up aboveground...

No one would be able to stand in their way. We have to defeat them here...

That had always been the plan. She had no intention of letting anyone in Silver Sword die.

"Just thinking about it is getting me excited! We've got to devour these offerings quick and get up above." Viena's attitude flipped right around from her earlier boredom, and then that big silver bow appeared again in her hands.

"...Alina." Jade, who had been silent for a while, finally opened his mouth. "Their god cores are pretty small. I bet they're two halves of a single core... From what I can tell, that means their attack power and durability are lower than Silha's individually."

"Yeah, I agree."

Though they lacked Silha's strength and durability, the twin dark gods could endlessly regenerate as long as their counterpart remained. Silver Sword would never win against them by taking the brute-force approach, as they had with Silha.

"Viena is after me," Jade said. "I'll draw her to me and lead her around. You take Fiena. We'll get them in a row, then destroy both cores at the same time with your war hammer... That's the best possible way to do it right now."

"You'll lead Viena around...? It's true her arrows are weaker than the weapons Silha used, but you obviously can't repel them with a Sigurth skill. If one of those girls gets a clean hit on you, you're dead."

"Don't worry about that. I have a plan."

"...Oh really? Okay, then."

"Let's go!"

With that cry, Jade and Alina leaped forward, racing in opposite directions.

33

From behind a rock, Lululee anxiously watched Alina and Jade's fight.

"Skill Activate: *Sigurth Wall*!"

Jade raced out and made the first move. That being said, he was just pulling out his usual skill.

But wait.

Jade took a knee and placed his hand on the ground, deploying *Sigurth Wall* there.

"Huh...?!"

He'd conferred his hardening skill to a completely pointless area, making it shine with a dim red glow. Jade rolled to avoid the arrow that came flying right after, then put his hand on the ground again when he had the chance.

"Sigurth Wall!"

He activated the same Sigurth skill over and over. After that, he kept dodging arrows as he fruitlessly activated his skill again and again, like he had before. By the time he was finished, he'd placed four red glowing points where he had activated *Sigurth Wall* on the floor of the cave.

Why would he do something like that...?

Lululee furrowed her brow. Normally, you would never activate the same skill multiple times concurrently—in fact, you couldn't. The use of the skill would exhaust you very quickly, stripping you of your ability to fight. Plus, even with Jade's powers of endurance, continuing to maintain four Sigurth activations would wear him out quickly.

"With an inferior ability like that, you won't be able to block my attack no matter how many times you fire it off, Mr. Cutie!" Viena laughed at Jade as she fired an arrow. The silver projectile plunged into the ground at his feet just as he barely moved out of the way, sending water splashing from a puddle. At the same time...

"Skill Activate: *Sigurth Blood*!" Jade stretched out his hand and activated his second skill.

"Wha—?" Lululee's heart stopped for a moment when she heard the name of that skill.

Sigurth Blood forced all attacks targeted at one's allies onto the caster. It was a self-sacrificing skill for getting out of the worst situations where Jade converted his body into a shield to protect his party members. He had promised that he would only use it in combination with Lululee's *Sigurth Revive*.

And it was true that she had cast *Sigurth Revive* on him, but Viena's attacks had only been directed at Jade to begin with—there didn't seem to be any point in using the skill at this juncture.

"Enough with your fruitless struggling."

Viena slipped soundlessly in front of Jade. Even if she wasn't as fast as Silha, she was still superhuman. Additionally, Jade was moving slower than usual since he was worn out from so many skill activations. The petite dark god effortlessly zoomed in on Jade.

"!"

"Jade!"

Viena had pointed an arrowhead directly between his eyes, close enough that he couldn't dodge. The moment Lululee let out a shriek...

"Converge!" Jade chanted something strange. "Deploy!"

A grating sound rang out, as if the very air was exploding.

At the same time, there came a burst of intense red skill light, bright enough to make you close your eyes. The source of the light was the four randomly conferred spots of *Sigurth Wall*.

"?! What's that?"

"Composite Skill Activate—*Millia*!"

Viena's disconcerted cry was cut off by the sound of air bursting. In tandem with this, the violent red glow from the four different locations Jade had marked gathered on his shield. Enveloped by crimson light so bright it was gaudy, his shield easily repelled the arrow from Viena's Dia skill.

"A Sigurth skill...repelled a Dia skill?!" Lululee cried out in shock.

No wonder she was surprised. Dia skills were the highest rank of skill, so Sigurth skills shouldn't have counteracted them—Silver Sword had learned that lesson the hard way in their previous fight with Silha.

"What the heck...?!"

It seemed that even Viena was confounded at having her arrow blocked by Jade's skill, which she had looked down on as an inferior ability. She widened her large eyes even further at the strange sight, panicking and looking around. Red lights drifted about Jade as if a vast quantity of energy was ready to seep out, and the conflicting powers from the two types of skills produced bursts of purple lightning as they collided against each other.

"That's...!" Lowe cried out, suddenly realizing. Lululee had struck on the very same thing. That was the same skill Jade had activated at the guild training grounds a few days ago, calling it "dangerous special training." After performing it, he'd been hit with exhaustion so intense that he collapsed.

"Ngh...!"

To little surprise, Jade winced just like he had during his training session as he staggered forward. Though this technique could manifest as much or more power than a Dia skill, it clearly wore him out.

"There's no way you could block my attack with that inferior technique!"

But Viena had absolute confidence in her own power as a dark god, so her bewilderment at having her attacked blocked by an "inferior technique" created a brief opening. She cautiously backed away from Jade—and then something lightly tapped her from behind.

It was her counterpart's back.

"Fiena?"

This whole time, Alina had been pushing Fiena, leading her into this position. The pair of dark gods were lined up back-to-back. The moment Viena, her face stiffening up, finally realized what they were doing, Alina was already swinging her war hammer overhead and taking a huge step forward.

"Haaaaahhhhhhhhh!!"

She made a big windup and struck Fiena's face with the pointed end of her war hammer, mercilessly crushing it, god core and all. A dull sound rang out through the cave, and after smashing Fiena, the hammer kept going, reaching Viena just like Alina had meant from the start...

Until it didn't.

"Tsk."

With a frustrated click of her tongue, Alina retreated back to Jade's side. A silver arrow skimmed right past the end of her nose.

Alina watched as Fiena made strange, muffled sounds and regenerated.

"That was close!" Viena shouted, her voice ringing through the cave after she just barely evaded Alina's blow.

The twin dark gods stood there, unfazed.

34

"...No good, huh?" Jade muttered, a wrinkle forming on his brow.

The timing of their attacks had been perfect, but the war hammer must have slowed slightly after destroying Fiena's body, giving Viena a split second to evade...and her twin time to regenerate.

This brute-force move would probably have worked on an opponent who didn't have the next-level athleticism of a dark god. Silver Sword and Alina couldn't have been up against a tougher foe.

"Are you all right, Jade?" Alina glanced over at Jade, who was already drenched in sweat.

Though Jade could feel his strength seeping quickly away from the backlash of multiple skill use, he put on a tough front and nodded. "Yeah. I can still fight."

"So…what was that? That skill you used to repel her arrow?"

"It was a composite skill."

"A composite skill…?" Having never heard the term before, Alina furrowed her brow.

"It's something I just worked out on my own. By activating two skills at once, you can double the effects of *Sigurth Wall*…creating *Millia*."

Fundamentally speaking, the defensive power that *Sigurth Wall* could confer was fixed.

No matter how many times you recast it, the effects would not stack, and there was an upper limit to how much it could enhance defensive power. So ordinarily, it would never be able to withstand the attack power of a blow that surpassed the upper limit of its defenses—a Dia skill.

However, there was a single technique that could let him surpass that limit. It was a method only available to Jade, who possessed multiple skills and exceptional endurance—he could combine the skill with other skills to force a layering of the effects of *Sigurth Wall*.

He'd hit upon the idea of using *Sigurth Blood* to accomplish this.

Sigurth Blood forced all skills directed at his allies to himself. Technically speaking, however, it directed *all* skills around him to himself unconditionally. By taking advantage of *Sigurth Blood*'s special characteristic, he could point the *Sigurth Wall* castings he'd activated back on himself, allowing him to layer *Sigurth Wall* despite the fact that it couldn't ordinarily stack. The idea was that the more *Sigurth Wall*s were activated around him, the more his defense would be enhanced, enabling him to break through that upper limit.

Jade had conceptualized that foolhardy technique quite a while ago, and when he'd tested it out back then, he hadn't lasted a second. After passing out, he'd wound up bedridden for around a week.

"I tried a bunch of things, but I can only stay conscious for four *Sigurth Wall*s...but that's enough to work on a Dia skill...!"

It was a brute-force method for amplifying his defense, so to speak, that took advantage of his high endurance. But now, even Jade had the power to go toe to toe with a dark god. He was no longer the pathetic tank he'd been in the last battle with Silha, when he had left everything to Alina.

Letting out a breath and psyching himself up, Jade drew the longsword at his waist. "...One more time, Alina."

"Huh?"

"Now we know that it really is impossible for you to defeat both at the same moment on your own. This time, I'll get Viena. We take them out at the same instant, together."

"You will...?"

"On my signal, we'll both leap into action."

Jade wasn't going to explain the details since a feeling of lethargy was creeping up on him as they were standing there. He'd gone through his "special training" several times, so he knew how long he could continue using multiple skills at once before losing consciousness—and that wasn't much longer. He wanted to end this before he keeled over from skill overuse backlash.

"...Fine." Alina must have realized what Jade was trying to do, because she nodded without asking any questions.

Then they turned their eyes on their target once more and both dashed out at practically the same moment.

"Woooow, mister! I'm impressed how you blocked my arrows with an inferior skill like that!"

As Jade approached Viena, the little dark god put on a show of dramatic surprise, mocking him. Her confusion over Jade blocking her attack had quickly subsided; ultimately, she'd realized that with her regenerative abilities, Jade and Alina couldn't touch her or Fiena.

"But that's not enough to win!" Viena said, nocking a silver arrow and firing it at Jade. Jade leaped sharply to the right to evade it and boldly moved onward. When another arrow followed, he ducked to dodge, taking another step forward. Then he repelled the third arrow with his shield, drawing closer and closer to his target.

Continuing to surge forward, he took a big step into sword range. Instantly, Jade undid *Millia*, then thrust his shield at Viena, blocking her line of sight.

"?!"

In exchange for undoing the skill on his shield, he tensed his right arm and clenched his grip on his sword.

"Converge! Deploy!"

The scattered red lights were yanked toward Jade, instantly wrapping around his blade.

His sword, layered with many *Sigurth Wall*s, was colored crimson. That same instant, he burst into sweat from head to toe. It was as though his body was crying out in agony from his continuous skill activation. Feeling his heart pound violently enough to burst, Jade glanced over to Alina. That was their cue. Alina picked up on that, and their eyes met—she'd been waiting for her moment, so she dashed right into range of Fiena.

"*Millia!*" Jade thrust out his sword, bolstered by many layers of defensive enhancements—and the tip of his glowing bloodred blade pierced deeply into Viena's throat, core and all.

"Ngh...ah?!" Viena widened her eyes in shock at having her core easily pierced not by a Dia skill weapon but by a mere longsword.

Jade's sword was bolstered with layers of defensive enhancements from *Millia*—in other words, its physical hardness had increased to the point where it was less a blade and more an iron rod. But incredible hardness was a weapon in its own right. After repelling the dark god's arrows, Jade was certain that his *Millia*-enhanced sword would be able to pierce the god core.

"Kuh…!"

But Jade was hit with even more backlash than anticipated from activating a composite skill a second time. His whole body groaned, and he staggered on his feet for a moment. But somehow, he kept upright, pulling his sword out and backing away from Viena.

"Ah…ah…?"

A large crack in the half core at her neck, Viena staggered one step back, two. Neither her painful-looking wound nor her core, now bifurcated, began regenerating. Jade glanced over and saw that Alina had blasted away Fiena's core—and her face—with her war hammer.

"It worked…!"

Judging from how the dark god duo's regenerative powers weren't working, it seemed like Jade had managed to break the core at the same time as Alina.

He was thankful she had such an excellent sense for combat and tactics execution, even though she was just a receptionist. She had easily pulled off timing her attack to the same moment as Jade—that wasn't normally something you could just do on the spot. Her talents really were wasted on office work.

Regardless, now they had completely blocked the dark gods' regenerative powers. Uncharacteristically certain of his victory, Jade relaxed just a tad.

That was when it happened.

"Too baaaaad! ♪"

A silver arrow flew straight at Jade's face.

"?!"

It was going to hit him—but as he stood there frozen in horror, the arrow was smacked aside, right in front of him. Alina had saved him.

"Hold on a minute. I know we attacked simultaneously..." Alina sounded a bit tense as she came over to Jade. She was watching Fiena regenerate before their eyes while Viena, having repaired the damage to her core, was smiling with composure.

"That's sooo amazing, mister. I knew a cute guy like you would be different!"

"Wha...?"

The sight left Jade in shock. There was no question that he and Alina had attacked at the same time.

"Simultaneous attacks won't work...?!"

Why? Jade was confused. He could have sworn they'd gotten both their cores. Both dark gods should have died, but they'd still been able to use their regenerative ability somehow.

"But you know...it really stings to get beat up by a low-level spawn, even if he is cute." Viena was murmuring something. "It's humiliating, isn't it...? It's humiliating..."

A moment later, Viena turned her eyes on Aiden. "Give me an offering... More power... Gimme a technique!" She drew her bow at Aiden as if she were taking her frustrations out on him.

Noticing that with a gasp, Jade ran toward Aiden. He drew his sword and deflected the arrow with a deafening *clang*, but he'd failed to brace himself properly first, so he ended up being flung backward to the hard stone ground. Practically rolling, Jade called out to Lowe. "Take Aiden aboveground! He's in the way!"

"...!"

Aiden started saying something on reflex when Jade screamed that out.

But Aiden's expression immediately turned harsh, and he closed his mouth. His gaze wandered for a while, then landed on his allies' bodies. Ultimately, he couldn't get a word out, so he just weakly hung his head.

Now that Aiden realized the true nature of what he'd been

seeking, the hidden side of the allies he'd believed in, and the point-lessness of the plan he'd pinned his last hopes on, he was crushed.

"...Are you sure, leader?" Lowe asked in confirmation, just in case. Silver Sword would lose their black mage if he took Aiden up.

"If the dark gods get outside, Lowe...I'll be counting on you," Jade replied in lieu of an answer. He wasn't about to treat Lowe like a burden, but it was a fact that if someone was going to leave the front lines, then Lowe, who had no effective moves against dark gods, was the best choice.

"...I don't know if I can defeat them with my skills, either. Well, if that happens, leave it to me." And with that show of courage, Lowe slung Aiden over his shoulder and went up the stairs.

"Ahh! The offering ran away!" Viena's face went red as she stamped her feet in frustration. "I'm mad now...! Fiena...!" Angry at how nothing had been going her way, Viena called out sharply to her counterpart.

Fiena came up to her twin as ordered, feet tapping on the stone floor. A beat later, Viena was mercilessly thrusting her nails into her throat, gouging out the little god core that was embedded in there.

"Wha—?! What is she...?!"

Without her god core, Fiena's body crumbled away and vanished.

Viena didn't even stop to watch her twin expire, her face twisted with rage as she swallowed the stolen god core. "You...made me mad..." The girl's low voice rang out eerily in the cave.

"Die...die...die...!" Viena muttered under her breath as her body began to swell.

"?!"

Her cute little face and hands ballooned before their eyes, losing all traces of girlishness. Jade stiffened at the bizarre sight; he couldn't understand what was happening in front of them.

"...Wha—?"

Eventually, a woman with brilliant golden hair appeared.

But she was about twice as tall as a normal human—big enough that the silver great bow that the girls had carried seemed small in her hands. She was expressionless, with hollow eyes and a slack jaw. And at her neck, a giant core even larger than Silha's shined with an eerie black luster.

There was a *zip* as a strong gale passed Jade's ear.

"Huh...?" A foolish-sounding noise slipped from his mouth.

That hadn't been the wind. It was one of the giantess's silver arrows.

A beat passed.

Then a violent crunch resounded from the rocky area near Jade. It was the sound of the arrow hitting the rocks and digging deep. The silver projectile was unable to withstand the speed with which it had been fired and fell apart.

Jade's breath caught as he watched this out of the corner of his eye.

He hadn't been able to see it.

He hadn't been able to move a single step.

He hadn't even been able to sense its presence.

It was pure coincidence that the arrow had punctured the earth instead of his head.

"I am Vilfina...," the giantess muttered sluggishly. But she moved with precision, and next she pointed her arrowhead at Alina and said quietly, "Die."

35

A shiver raced down Alina's spine.

The arrow fired by the giant woman who called herself Vilfina made a ferocious shrieking noise as it tore through the air toward her. It was so fast that it headed for Alina in a straight line instead of an arc.

"—!"

Alina's mind went blank for an instant in the face of the arrow's tremendous speed, but she forced herself to snap out of it and raised her war hammer practically on reflex to defend herself. The silver arrow's aim was true and struck her weapon.

And then a weak *whoosh* sound rang out.

"...Huh...?!"

Alina's eyes widened as she stared at the sight in front of her.

Moments ago, she'd repelled the dark gods' arrows with ease. But now, Vilfina's arrow plunged into her weapon in the blink of an eye...

It had destroyed her war hammer.

And the brutal arrow still didn't stop there, its trajectory changing only slightly to dig into Alina's side.

"—!!"

Stabbing pain seized her entire body.

As her field of vision constricted, the remains of her silver war hammer burst into silver particles and scattered. Alina had never seen such a thing before, and it sent her thoughts screeching to a halt.

She was thrown backward and rolled across the ground.

"K-kah..."

She'd only taken an arrow to her side, but her entire body was wracked with immense pain. It hurt so badly, she felt like she was going to pass out. Her thoughts swirled as the woman who had called herself Vilfina lumbered toward her, holding an arrow right in her hand.

"I am Vilfina... Die... I am Vilfina...," she muttered as she raised the silver arrow over the fallen receptionist.

36

"Alina!!"

Just as the giantess slammed down the silver arrow over Alina, Jade leaped in at the last moment, grabbing Alina and rolling away to avoid taking a hit.

"Gah…!"

In the process, the arrow skimmed Jade's upper arm. Despite only grazing him, the projectile easily penetrated his armor, digging into flesh and carving a deep wound. Having failed to capture its prey, the arrowhead plunged into the hard rock ground and made an eerie *tnk* noise, gouging a deep hole. Jade staggered at the shock of the impact, but he got away from Vilfina, Alina in his arms.

"What the heck is she…?!"

Vilfina slowly lifted her head; she looked unsightly, like some sort of botched human. She must have lost sight of Jade, as she scanned around the area a bunch of times with vacant eyes.

She was terrifically powerful but moved slowly, like a low-intellect monster. Figuring out this much, Jade carried Alina to Lululee.

"Ah, Alina…!" Lululee blanched as well as she raced up to Alina. "She's avoided a fatal injury… But this wound…it's strange…"

Jade lay Alina down while keeping a wary eye on Vilfina, who was lumbering toward them, his face twisting in agony from the wound.

Jade's arm wasn't bleeding, even though it had been cut deep enough to slice an artery; instead, the wound was all black. And on top of that, the *Sigurth Revive* cast on Jade wasn't working. The healing wasn't kicking in at all.

"Is it not a normal wound…?"

It hurt so badly that it was as if there was something writhing and raging around inside the wound. Alina was also in such intense pain that her forehead had burst into sweat, and she was clenching her teeth like she was in agony.

Is that also from…?

Jade looked over at the giantess and furrowed his brow. The large woman, staring into space as though her thoughts were frozen, did have a giant god core at the base of her neck. Carved on each of her cheeks were the half marks of Dia, the two lining up eerily.

He thought back to what Viena had said proudly on many occasions: *"We are two as one."* When combined together, the half marks of Dia inscribed on both her cheeks did indeed create a single magic sigil.

Is that hulking creature the twin dark gods' true form…?!

Vilfina had the mark of Dia and a giant black god core. Purely in terms of her characteristics, that did indeed make her a dark god. But she was clearly different from Silha—he'd possessed thoughts and feelings, but Vilfina was like another entity entirely, one which just so happened to resemble a human being.

"Heal!"

Seeing that *Sigurth Revive* wasn't working on Jade, Lululee cast her healing magic on Alina. But of course, if even a Sigurth skill wouldn't work on the wound, there was no way that magic, which was even weaker, would be effective.

"Minoos!" Still not giving up, she tried another spell. But that didn't work, either. "It seems like…it's not poison…but magic doesn't work at all, either…!"

"Heh-heh, it's no use. My shots are arrows of death!" came Viena's voice.

Unbeknownst to Silver Sword, Vilfina had vanished, and the twins had returned to their separate forms.

Viena was hopping around in joy, laughing at the consternation of Jade's party. "This move directly confers death itself, you know. If it so much as skims you, you're a goner! Once a bit of time elapses, certain death awaits. ♪"

"C-certain death…?!"

"Right? That's why I told you, it's boring! I'd rather have some kinda fancy move that goes like *boom*! Agh, they just don't understand a maiden's heart." Viena put her hands on her hips in a deliberate manner, acting cutely angry.

But there was nothing cute about the reality that she had presented them with.

Oh—so that arrow wasn't just a ranged weapon.

Jade was struck speechless as he finally realized why *Sigurth Revive* wasn't working on him. The arrow conferred the Dia skill effect of certain death on the target it touched. In other words, it was a Dia skill–level status effect. That was why *Sigurth Revive*, a lower-level skill, had no impact.

Their fortunes had done an abrupt about-face, and now they were in deep trouble.

Beyond that, just who was that Vilfina woman? Jade hadn't sensed any intellect in her empty, unfocused eyes or in the way that she muttered the same thing deliriously, but on the other hand, she was ludicrously strong.

She destroyed Alina's war hammer...?!

When they had fought the dark god Silha before, Alina's strength had been even with his. So was this one an even more powerful god?

Whatever the case, at this rate, Alina would...

"Lululee. Undo the *Sigurth Revive* you have cast on me and invest all your efforts into healing Alina. I'm leaving it to you to undo the certain death status on her...!"

Jade knew that wouldn't be possible, but he said it anyway. He had to say that. Lululee just had to pull it off for him somehow.

"..."

Lululee looked down at Alina, moaning in pain. She just gave a little nod, her face pale.

37

"The arrow of death hurts, doesn't it, Mr. Cutie?"

Viena had done a one-eighty from her earlier intense rage and was now in a great mood, humming along. Fiena, on the other hand, was as expressionless as before. The twin dark gods and Jade were facing off.

"You want to end it already, huh, mister?" The two of them slowly ambled up to Jade. The girls' eerie giggling echoed through the cave.

But Jade just snorted at them. "You're making a big mistake if you think pain can stop me."

Things were really bad—even though Jade was making snappy remarks, his neck was damp with sweat.

Alina's unknown wound had rattled him. His heart was pounding hard, and he was trying to rein in his thoughts, but they wouldn't stop racing.

A simultaneous attack wouldn't work. And when the twins had transformed into Vilfina, even Alina's *Dia Break* hadn't harmed her. Jade had already activated his composite skill twice, so he couldn't keep this up much longer.

"Ngh…!"

Just then, everything turned upside down. He heard his sword clatter to the ground, and after experiencing a strange, floaty sensation, he was on his knees.

"Jade!" Lululee cried out in a panic behind him.

Belatedly, he realized that his legs had given out, and he was on his hands and knees on the cold floor of the cave. The metallic taste of blood was spreading inside his mouth. Then Jade saw the red light of *Millia* vanish from his out-of-reach longsword, and everything clicked.

This is my limit…!

It was a miracle that he hadn't passed out, like he did during training.

"Shit..." Even his swear came out weak.

What am I supposed to do...when I'm like this...?!

He didn't know what he should do to win. He had no idea.

No—maybe it was no use.

For the first time in Jade's life as an adventurer and a tank, he felt his spirit about to break.

"Is that it for you, Mr. Cutie? I was thinking about taking your soul, but..." Viena curled her lips like a devil and raised her bow, shifting her aim slightly from Jade. The arrowhead that brought certain death was now pointed—at Alina.

"That offering has been really annoying, trying to hide from me, so I'll get her first. I'll take my time eating you later, Mr. Cutie. ♪"

"...!"

Jade's heart pounded in his chest.

He no longer had *Millia* to block an arrow. If Viena fired an arrow now, it was over.

Alina was going to die.

Alina was...

...Calm down...!

Jade took a deep breath.

Lululee was sure to heal Alina. So until she did, he had to do whatever he could to defend the two women to the last. That was the only chance they had of winning, so he just had to put all his strength into doing what he could.

And as a tank, that meant...drawing aggro away from Alina.

Crawling along the ground, Jade desperately watched Viena, thinking of what he could do to get her attention.

The twin dark gods, their childish appearance, the way their bodies weren't as powerful or durable as Silha's, their unlimited regenerative powers, the way they each had half a core and half a mark of Dia.

...Half?

By the time it hit Jade, his mouth was already open.

"Hold up—you *failure...!*"

Viena was just about to fire when her hand froze. "...What did you just say, mister?"

"You didn't hear me? I called you a failure."

Spitting blood, straining all his limbs, Jade got to his feet. This was an all-or-nothing provocation.

Tanks put themselves on the line to protect their allies—they could never let someone else take the aggro.

That was the heart and soul of being a tank. Using Hastor to pull aggro worked on monsters since they acted on instinct, but it had no effect on humans since they could think and act on reason. Of course, that went the same for the dark gods.

But magic wasn't the only way to capture aggro.

Insults that would rattle a target's emotions, skillful bluffs... Those tactics worked precisely because they took advantage of an opponent's feelings.

"If the time comes, use any means you can to secure aggro. Even if you're stripped naked, draw the enemy's attention, use your head, and don't rely on magic." His tanking teacher had told him that countless times.

"Hey, mister. I *really* hate those kinds of brain-dead provocations, you know."

"You think this is just a provocation?"

"Huh?"

"It's common for a number of failures to be created in the process of reaching a completed product," Jade began speaking dispassionately, ignoring Viena's icy, murderous aura. What he was about to say now was all just speculation, without any basis at all. He didn't even know if it was enough to draw the attention of the twin gods.

But he absolutely would keep his hold on the aggro.

"It's our understanding that all objects marked with the sun sigil, the mark of Dia, have functionality beyond imagination. We don't know anything about them, aside from that they were made by the ancients... But there's just one thing that I can say: I've never once seen a mark of Dia that was half missing."

"..."

Viena forgot about aiming at Alina, just staring at Jade. She'd been expressive as a child before, but now her face had stiffened up as she pasted on an inhuman expression like that of a doll.

"The half mark of Dia on your faces—if you're two as one, then why is it that when you became Vilfina, it didn't become a perfect, singular Dia mark?"

Two as one—if that was how it was, then Viena should have become complete when she'd eaten Fiena's core. But their fusion had created Vilfina, who possessed only strength and no intellect. The mark of Dia had still not become whole; she'd just gained half a sigil on each cheek.

"The mark of Dia was what the ancients carved into their creations. So then what does a half mark of Dia mean?"

"..."

"I've met one other dark god besides you two. He had a complete mark of Dia carved on him, and your functionality is clearly inferior to his. You can regenerate, but your bodies are weak, and Vilfina is powerful but unintelligent. It's all lacking a bit, here and there."

"...A failure? No...," Viena muttered finally.

But Jade went on, ignoring her protests. "So this is what I figured—maybe you were implanted with *unsuccessful* cores that were created via trial and error before reaching a completed product. You can combine two failures, but that doesn't make a success. Vilfina is just a mishmash of mistakes. No—maybe I should say that forcing the cores together makes it even more unstable—a piece of trash that's difficult to control?"

"No...!"

"You aren't two as one. You're two defective creations that both have slightly inferior functionality. That's why the people who made you, the ancients, carved those half sigils on your bodies—as proof that you're failed projects."

"Shut up!!" Viena's shrill voice echoed fiercely in the cave.

Her eyes were wide with rage, her expression stiff, and her face bloodlessly pale, her eyes alone bloodshot and flashing as she glared at Jade like she was ready to bite.

All traces of the charming little girl she'd been before had vanished.

"No... No...nonononononono...!!" Viena cried out, clutching her head in her hands. Her eyes wavered intensely and burned with rage as she glared at Jade. She pointed at him, finger trembling from intense emotion. "Calling me a failure...when you're just an offering... I'll eat you...! I'll chop you into bits... I'll make you experience the worst pain imaginable...!"

"Unfortunately, I'm already hurting all over."

Eyes fixed on the shaking arrowhead that was pointed right at him, Jade smiled.

He'd gotten her aggro.

"I'm not giving you my life so easily, though...!" Raising his shield, Jade yelled, "Converge...deploy!"

There was that strange bursting sound, and then his field of vision went white for an instant. The moment he tried to activate his skill, intense pain ran through his whole body. It hurt so bad that he trembled. Literal fireworks of blood were shooting out of him.

"*Ngk...*"

It was the backlash to his third composite skill activation.

The symptoms were worse than expected, but Jade didn't flinch—since the time he'd made up his mind to use this composite skill in battle against a dark god, he'd been fully aware that he would suffer more than just a little backlash.

Combined with the wound from the arrow of death in his arm,

he was in intense pain. He wasn't even sure where the sensation was coming from anymore, but he used his iron will to push down the agony assaulting his entire body. He just about staggered, but he forced himself to brace, biting his lip to restrain the urge to pass out from pain.

Heedless, Jade continued. "Composite skill, activate."

A frustrating memory from not so long ago flickered through his mind.

He'd been helpless in the face of the strange and powerful foe that was the dark god Silha.

Alina had been in danger, but he hadn't been able to move at all.

This time around, he hadn't been able to let Alina fully enjoy the Centennial Festival that she'd been looking forward to for so long. *It's because I'm not strong enough to oppose a dark god—because in a battle against one, I have no choice but to rely on her.*

He wanted the power to be able to fight evenly against a dark god. He wanted to be the kind of man who could give Alina the peace that she wanted. She'd looked so happy during the Centennial Festival. If she could always have a smile like that…

If it was for her, it didn't matter how much his body tore apart.

"Millia!!"

There was a burst of red in his flickering field of view. Jade couldn't even tell anymore if it was the color of blood or the light of his skill, but it no longer mattered. He forced the corners of his lips upward, raised his bloodred shield, and gave Viena a daring grin.

"Come fire that arrow at me. Try and kill me, if you can."

38

"J-Jade…!" Lululee cried out quietly as she watched him activate his composite skill for the third time.

Viena and Fiena were yelling curses as they lost themselves to fury and fired arrows at Jade. But he was repelling all of them with his shield. Every deflection made a terrible clang that gave Lululee shivers. The blood drained from her face as she observed that nightmarish scene.

The light of Jade's composite skill hung in the air, swimming around the cave. Lululee watched on in terror.

"...!"

She was afraid. She had no way to meet Jade's expectations, even though he was giving himself up to protect them, shaving down his life while believing in her.

Heal Alina? How should she do that?

Lululee looked down at Alina in a daze.

The wound in her side was all black, as though it was eating away at her. Alina's face was as pale as a corpse's.

Since Alina possessed a Dia skill, a lower-ranked skill like *Sigurth Revive* would not activate on her. Even if it had, judging from how her ability hadn't worked on Jade's wound, it wouldn't be useful regardless. White magic wouldn't work, either.

But she had to heal her.

Think. Think. Think. Think. Think. Think.

But Lululee thoughts were completely out of order, and she could neither come up with a way to get out of this situation nor sift through all her healing knowledge for a solution. Instead, she just kept focusing on an unrelated memory.

It was a vision so familiar that it made her nauseous—the scene of having driven her old party to their deaths.

The similarly hopeless situation in front of her made Lulu think of the past, forcing her to a standstill.

It's no use. I just can't do it. I just don't have the power to get us through this.

I'm helpless.

I'm incompetent.

I'm going to lose my party again, and it's all my fault.

A dry *katunk* rang out. It was the sound of her rod slipping from her slack hand.

"...I...I'm sorry...Alina...Jade...!"

Lululee bit her lip; at some point, she'd started crying. On this battlefield where life and death hung in the balance, worthless water streamed ineffectually from her eyes.

"I can't do it...I just can't do it... I can't...do anything...," she whined feebly, hanging her head and crying in the face of this wound she couldn't do anything about.

I'm sorry I can't do anything.

I'm sorry, I'm sorry, I'm sorry—

"It's fine."

A quiet voice came down to her.

When Lululee lifted her head with a start, Alina was pressing her wound and trying to get to her feet.

Seeing that, she forgot her despair and leaped up. "Ah, Alina, you can't move! Your wound...!"

"It doesn't matter. I have to win, or we'll die... If you think up some good idea, then you can heal me then."

"Th...that's not what I mean! I just...I just can't...!"

"Listen." Alina exhaled heavily like she was psyching herself up and thrust a shaking hand in front of Lululee. Even with the possibility of her death before her, there was no fear in her eyes. No—something even more desperate and dazzling blazed deep in her irises. "I don't want to lose anyone in my life."

"...Huh...?"

"Not even that guy." Alina had fixed her gaze on Jade. "I'll fight for that. It doesn't matter if it hurts or if there aren't any heals."

"...!"

"Skill Activate: *Dia Break*...!" Alina grimaced in pain. But when her war hammer appeared, she clasped it tightly.

Lululee said nothing, just stared in bewilderment.

Why didn't you heal us?

The things Aiden had said continued to torment her, stabbing her heart. But Alina had refuted those words. She was saying it was fine if she didn't get healed.

"I'll fight for my own sake. That's all."

How can she be like this?

Lululee was in shock. She had thought of Alina so simplistically—as someone with a strong skill, as someone who struggled with overtime, as an amazing person who could do what an adventurer did despite being a receptionist—that now she was embarrassed she'd ever thought that way.

Alina was going to fight to the end. Surely, no matter what situation she was driven into, no matter how badly wounded she was, she would continue to fight on—because she wanted to save the things that were important to her.

"…!"

What am I doing?

Lululee clenched her fist. Her tears had stopped.

At some point, Lululee had started relying entirely on *Sigurth Revive*. That was why she had lost confidence so easily when Silha had turned her skill back on her.

Lululee's failure had resulted in her old party members sustaining injuries or dying, but she'd shamelessly kept plugging away as a healer because she wouldn't be able to bear the alternative. She hadn't wanted her last deed as a healer to be murder.

She'd wanted to get stronger.

"…Alina!"

Before Lululee knew what she was doing, she was holding Alina back. She picked up her fallen staff, wiped at the tears left on her face with her sleeve, and said to Alina, "Please wait here. I *will* heal that wound…!"

Alina turned around to see Lululee's resolute expression and widened her eyes for an instant. Then she turned toward Jade for a moment in hesitation, but seeing the blazing determination deep in Lululee's eyes, she gave a little nod. "…Okay."

Alina was practically falling over as she leaned against the wall. Sweat was beading on her neck, and her face was pale—she had just been putting on a strong front.

Next, Lululee called out to her party leader. "Jade! Please give me a little more time. I'll heal Alina."

"…Roger!"

Lululee hated *Sigurth Revive*, the ability she'd been granted.

It hadn't manifested when her allies had been on the brink of death. It hadn't been useful when it had mattered most.

That was why she had never tried to learn more about it. She had never thought about the possibilities it could offer. She hadn't, for instance, even tested whether double casting it would stack.

But Jade and Lowe had been watching over Lululee all this time. Alina had forgiven Lululee for being so stupid and giving up on trying to heal her.

So Lululee wanted to save them—this time, for sure.

There was a limit to what people could do. That was true. But she didn't want to use that as an excuse to give up on the lives of the friends that were dear to her. If there was no way forward, then she should just make a new one. Jade had pulled it off, so she should be able to do it, too.

"Don't you worry about me." Jade sounded somehow glad to hear Lululee's assertion. "I'll keep you both safe while you're treating her. You focus on healing."

"Okay."

Even a Sigurth skill, if it was reapplied, could become equal to a Dia skill. *Sigurth Revive* was a powerful healing skill that would keep whoever it was conferred to in an able-bodied state. It also cured status effects. If *Sigurth Revive* could reduplicate, then by layering it on a target, Lululee should be able to erase the "certain death" status effect that had been conferred to Alina via a Dia skill. She had no choice but to bet on that possibility.

If Lululee's guess was wrong, or if she ran out of strength before she finished casting, or if she failed, then it would all be over. Alina would die, along with Jade, Lowe, and everyone in Iffole.

But she *would* do it.

"Skill Activate: *Sigurth Revive!*"

Putting her hands to Alina's blackened wound, Lululee activated her skill. The red light of the Sigurth skill gushed out, but within seconds, it was quashed by the black darkness and weakly faded away.

But before the light of the skill was completely extinguished, Lululee used it a second time. "Skill Activate: *Sigurth Revive!*" The ability surged out once more, tearing undauntedly into the dark god's Dia skill.

Her vision wavered.

Lululee was assaulted by a feeling of lethargy she'd never experienced before; it was like someone had tied lead around her entire body. Her strength was rapidly being drained away. That was clear to her. Sweat burst from her every pore, and her heart started racing.

This was beyond what could be described as *exhaustion*. There was clearly something wrong with her. But Alina's wound was still not healed. *Sigurth Revive*, which she'd cast twice, was starting to disappear, too.

"Sk…ill Activate…! *Sigurth Revive!!*"

Please. Please work.

Lululee prayed to the gods and activated her skill for the third time. She was assaulted by an even sharper dizziness than before. Her consciousness was muddled and growing dim, but she dug her nails into the hard rock and desperately kept herself awake. *Jade's been withstanding pain like this until now? Ahh, I haven't accomplished anything. I hate* Sigurth Revive *so much, but I've been relying on it entirely.*

"...I can't give in...!"

If a party's healer gave up, then it was all over.

"Skill Activate: *Sigurth Revive*!!"

Now was the time, and Lululee went for it again. The red light of her Sigurth skill grew denser before her eyes. The palm of her outstretched hand felt hot enough to burn. Her breathing came fast and hard, and she wasn't getting enough air. She felt like she was suffocating.

But she couldn't give up. She could never give up. Because only a healer could cure her comrade's wounds.

Out of the corner of her eye, she saw that the red light had started to push back the darkness, just a little.

"Skill Activate: *Sigurth Revive*!!"

This is my duty!

39

With Aiden slung over his shoulder, Lowe ascended the dark stairs that led to the surface.

"Shit, why is this happening...?! I just wanted a Dia skill," Aiden muttered. He'd been complaining to himself for a while. He was being selfish, but Lowe didn't get angry at him or argue back, just silently ignored him as he focused on getting up aboveground. Right now, Lowe just had to take Aiden away from this dungeon.

"It's her fault... That murderer ruined my life...!" Aiden went on.

"Agh, come on. You're being obnoxious."

But as soon as they crossed over the magic-frozen lake and reached the shore, Lowe sighed and shoved the man away.

"...?!"

Aiden hastily got to his feet, but then his expression stiffened;

Lowe had thrust his rod right at his nose. Before Lowe's piercing gaze and magic rod, Aiden swallowed what he'd been about to say.

"You've been grumbling to yourself all this time—but you've got it all wrong, you moron," said Lowe.

"…What's wrong about what I said?! My party died because of that murderer! I lost my right arm! And my eye! If that had never happened, then I wouldn't have been forced into this pathetic—"

Aiden was unable to continue, because Lowe had closed his mouth. No, that was putting it too lightly. Lowe had grabbed hold of Aiden's cheeks so hard that his nails dug into his skin, drawing blood and forcing his mouth shut.

"Ah…agh…!"

"Talk smack about Lululee one more time with that filthy mouth of yours, and I'll crush half your face."

"…!"

That was how far Lowe had needed to go to finally make Aiden see things clearly.

Despite the mage consistently staying out of Lululee's business, his eyes were now seething with rage. His murderous intent was so fierce it sent chills down Aiden's spine.

Aiden felt incredible fear beneath Lowe's gaze. He had no real basis for this, but he knew that the look in the mage's eyes was clearly abnormal. Lowe wasn't staring at Aiden like he would a person or living thing with the eyes of a seasoned adventurer.

If anything, Lowe was wearing the blood-soaked gaze of a killer, of a man completely familiar with murder.

"Wh-what are you—?!" Aiden couldn't help but ask while trembling, so scared that he forgot the pain in his cheek. "Are you really an adventurer…?!"

"I'm under no obligation to reply to you." Lowe dismissed Aiden's question and continued dispassionately. "Listen, I'm a gentleman, so I won't be so crass as to criticize someone else's past. And I never gave a damn about what's done, about who's at fault and who isn't. But…"

Lowe paused a moment, then continued quietly. "…Lululee never ran from being a healer. She never turned away from her weakness. But you, on the other hand, tried to turn to something strong—I don't care if it was a Dia skill or whatever—to avoid owning up to your faults."

"…!"

"It would be easy to cut you to pieces right now, but that would just make Lululee cry. She'd feel regret, even over a scumbag like you. So whatever. If you aren't gonna grow up and stop acting like a spoiled brat, then don't ever show your filthy face to Lululee ever again…!" Lowe shoved Aiden away, then started walking for the forest exit without another glance.

"I'm gonna go call for backup from guild headquarters. If the dark god comes up top, no matter how many people are up here, it's over. Unlike Lululee, I'm not so kind as to waste my time on a loser like you."

"…"

"Go ahead and run or whatever," Lowe spat.

Behind him, he sensed Aiden hesitate, then vanish into the woods. After listening to him go, Lowe headed for guild headquarters.

****

A burst of bright red light from a Sigurth skill momentarily dyed the pale blue cave crimson.

"!" Lululee's breath caught.

Her repeated *Sigurth Revives* had eaten up all the *Dia Morte* conferred by the dark god. At the same time, it had healed Alina's damaged organs, connected her severed muscle fibers, and reformed her torn skin, closing her grievous wound.

The darkened area on Alina's body gradually narrowed, then vanished. Then, as if it had used up all its strength, the red skill light of *Sigurth Revive* also melted away.

But the hole in Alina's cloak now showed unwounded skin, perfectly restored.

"I...I did it...!" Lululee breathed.

Sigurth Revive could stack. As Lululee hazily digested that fact, she was grateful for her skill for the very first time. Her shoulders were heaving, her whole body was soaked with sweat, and she was chilled to her core, but she was filled with a sense of accomplishment.

"I cured Alina..." Lululee raised her voice, feeling somewhat proud. Before she knew it, she was shaking the unconscious receptionist by the shoulders. "Alina! Alina?"

But no matter how many times Lululee called out to her, Alina's heavy lids did not move.

"...Huh?" It couldn't be—had she not made it in time?

Had the certain death conferred by *Dia Morte* already come to pass? Lululee widened her eyes. Her heart was ice as it fluttered in her chest.

"Alina! Please get up! I don't want you to die, Alina—!" Lululee yelled. Just then, her vision wavered. Heaven and earth flipped, and before she knew it, she had collapsed atop Alina's stomach. "Ah..."

It was the backlash from skill overuse. *Not at a time like this.* Though her hands could barely move, Lululee desperately tried to pull Alina up into a sitting position. But darkness was slowly creeping over her vision.

"Ali...na..."

And then Lululee passed out.

40

Jade's consciousness was fading.

He didn't know how much time had passed since Lululee had begun healing Alina, but Alina still showed no signs of giving up, and he hadn't heard from the desperate white mage since then, either.

But Jade believed in Lululee. The problem was that his body couldn't hold out any longer.

"Goff!"

He was spitting blood again. Clearly, he was being hit with backlash from having repeatedly activated his composite skill. Blood was oozing here and there, and his body felt like it was burning. After a certain point, however, he'd also started feeling frozen to the core. He had experienced this sensation a few times now—this was proof of oncoming death. Things were finally getting bad.

Ah, I'm gonna pass out...

Jade's mind clouded over for an instant. The next moment, he came to his senses and saw an arrowhead appear before him, as though he'd warped forward through time. Just as Jade realized he'd passed out for a moment, one of those terrifying arrows that brought death with just a touch was inches from his face...

****

I have to go.

Alina suddenly thought, feeling floaty, like in a dream.

She felt like she'd been in a very bad situation just a moment ago, but she couldn't remember why. Instead, an old memory came to her. She had to go. But where?

Oh yes. To the Centennial Festival.

Alina's burning desire to attend the Centennial Festival had bloomed in her second year as a receptionist. That had been right in the middle of the Centennial Festival Special Bonus Period.

"Huh?! You don't know about the Centennial Festival, miss?" a chatty adventurer who had come to her reception window asked with exaggerated surprise. "It's going on right now!"

"I see. I'm not particularly interested."

"You should try going, even if it's just for the third day! It's real pretty!"

I have to do overtime again because of you guys, though…!

Cursing the adventurer in her mind while struggling to keep her feelings off her face, Alina went about stiffly processing the quest.

All the while, the chatty adventurer kept endlessly flapping his lips. "For the big event on the third day, there's this thing called the soul's rest ceremony. The magic lights are so, like, *whoo* in the sky. It's so pretty, it makes fireworks look like nothing."

"The soul's rest ceremony?"

"Yup. It's a service for the souls of departed adventurers."

"That's a pretty depressing thing to do during a festival."

"We mourn them by partying over the course of the event to keep it from being depressing. It's beautiful. Iffole's famous for it."

"Uh-huh."

Being famous for people's souls… Just what were adventurers thinking? They really were idiots.

But if you die, you're dead. That's all there is to it.

Alina remembered the adventurer who had died in a dungeon when she had been small—Shroud. Alina had loved him, and she had loved adventurers, too. She had dreamed of one day becoming an adventurer and heading out together with Shroud to conquer a dungeon.

But reality was cruel.

One day, Shroud was attacked by monsters in a dungeon, and he exited Alina's life just like that.

From then on, the consequences of choosing a profession as unstable and dangerous as adventuring, the consequences of filling your head with dreams and letting your guard down, and the immense cruelty of the world were engraved into young Alina's heart—along with a loneliness that would never be wiped away.

"I don't think doing something like that will make the dead happy." Before she knew it, those words had left her lips.

To begin with, the souls they were mourning had long since made the journey to heaven of their own accord. That wouldn't change whether the people left behind held a party to mourn them or cry for them. They weren't coming back.

The departed wouldn't be able to stand their deaths being used as plausible pretense for an event that attracted customers, either. If it were Alina, she would have definitely been mad.

"..." The adventurer blinked in shock for a moment at Alina's remark cold remark, but when he saw her dispassionately process his quest, he smirked. "Well, yeah, sure. That sort of thing is done to satisfy us, the survivors."

"...I see."

That was even more stupid. Engaging in this chitchat was a waste of her time. She wanted to see him off already and finish up the work she had piled up.

"Thank you very much for the wonderful conversation," she said. "The next person is waiting, so..."

"Ahh, sorry!"

After driving away the lingering adventurer with a by-the-book remark, Alina went back to battling the adventurers as they came surging forward again.

"...I'm tired..."

Later that night in the office after hours, Alina was lying face down on her desk by herself.

She could faintly hear the bustling of the celebration. Outside, the third day of the Centennial Festival was in full swing, and lights as bright as day were flickering out the window.

There was a mountain of documents left that she had to clean up, but she had no more motivation to do overtime, and she was completely exhausted. Alina was still unused to business at the reception window and dealing with talkative adventurers, so she felt pressure to avoid making mistakes. The day shift alone had used up all her strength.

"...The soul's rest ceremony, huh?"

For no particular reason, she found herself looking at a flyer for the Centennial Festival.

It turned out that the ceremony the adventurer had mentioned was the main event of the evening of the third day. People stuck magic balls of light into special bottles made using the technology of the ancients and gathered them at a special installation at the square. Then at the stroke of midnight, the bottles would melt away, and the magic lights would rise into the sky all at once.

Alina glanced at the clock and saw that it was just about midnight.

"..."

She was just a little curious. Plus, she was pooped from all her overtime. As though being sucked in, Alina headed for the window, opened the curtains, and turned her exhausted face to the sky.

"—!"

That moment, her breath caught.

Hundreds of lights were floating upward. Far more orbs than she could have ever imagined were being released, slowly spreading from every which way as they rose into the sky. Countless lights appeared between the buildings. As time passed, the glowing orbs filled the whole night sky to eventually become a ceiling of light that bobbed around in the darkness.

"Well, yeah, sure. That sort of thing is done to satisfy us, the survivors."

Even though she knew that it was pointless intellectually—her brain concluded that the ceremony was foolish, arbitrary, and meaningless—her heart trembled for some reason. The sight was so beautiful that she forgot to breathe.

She wanted to have Shroud's soul join theirs—that's what she felt.

Even if it was a foolish, arbitrary, and selfish thing to do.

She wanted to mourn him—his soul. For no one else but herself.

She wanted to accept the tragic reality that he was gone.

I have to go.

Suddenly, it all came back to Alina.

That's right, I have to go. So that I won't lose someone dear to me again. Because the battle with the dark gods was not yet over.

41

The arrow headed straight for Jade's face, but just as it was about to plunge into him, it flew off into another direction with a *crack*. Something had leaped in at the last minute to repel the arrow.

Jade lifted his face with a start to see a familiar profile. "...Alina..."

He didn't even know if the words had come out right. His mouth was filled with blood, so for all he knew, he might have just made a strange gurgling noise. Nevertheless, he curled his lips into a smile. Lululee had done it. She had healed Alina, just like she'd said she would.

Alina scowled like always and stared at Jade. "Why is it when I take my eyes off you for a moment, you wind up on death's door...?"

"Guys look cool when they're covered in wounds..."

"They really don't."

"Hey, Alina—" The moment Jade relaxed, he tipped over. That wouldn't do—this was the important part. But his body was completely sapped of strength.

"A tank really shouldn't be saying something like this, but..." With his last energy, Jade held up his right palm. "Can I leave the rest to you?"

"Yeah. Nice work." With that short reply, Alina smacked her palm against Jade's. Her hand was small and soft, and the sensation of it was so delicate that he felt frustration well up inside him at having to rely on it again.

"...Counting on you—"

And that was the last thing Jade was aware of before he blacked out.

42

Jade swayed and keeled over right past Alina's side to fall over with a splat.

"..."

After that, he didn't even twitch. If he was this worn down, he must have activated his composite skill a third time. Without that, there was no way the dark gods would have given them time for Alina to be healed.

When Alina had awoken, Lululee was collapsed beside her. She must have pushed herself to the limit to heal Alina.

"Why...are you alive?" Viena had a completely different air about her now and was consumed by a dark wrath. She bared her teeth upon seeing Alina. Fiena watched along quietly from her twin's side with emotionless eyes. "Didn't my arrow take you out?"

"Not quite, so here I am."

Viena clicked her tongue with even greater irritation at Alina's nonanswer. But frankly speaking, Alina didn't know how Lululee had healed her wound, either. She had no way to answer.

"More importantly," Alina told her quietly, "we have some business to settle."

"...What's got you so full of yourself? You're weaker than me."

"Whether I'm full of myself or weaker than you, I'm still gonna do it," Alina said flatly, then held out her hand. A white magic sigil deployed soundlessly, and she took in hand the silver war hammer that appeared along with it.

"I want to end this quick and go back to the Centennial Festival, now that it's starting up again. You want to go up above and slaughter people. Only one side will get what they want..."

She glared at Viena. "...The side that survives."

43

"Ahh, shut up...shut up, shut up...! There's no way a mere offering could withstand my power!" Viena yelled at Alina, then called to Fiena.

She wants to become Vilfina again, Alina suddenly realized. Just then, she went after Fiena, who'd come running over to her twin. "I won't let you...!" Alina swung up her war hammer to prevent them from uniting.

Then quit.

Alina stopped flat, as Viena plucked out Fiena's core and tossed it in her mouth right before her eyes.

"Ah-ha-ha-ha-ha-ha! Do you finally get it? It doesn't matter what some piddling creature like you does!"

Laughing scornfully at Alina with her mouth wide, Viena transformed. Alina simply watched as her shadow squelched into the shape of a giant monster.

Eventually, the giant woman appeared. "I am Vilfina." She nocked an arrow to her great bow as her vacant eyes stared off somewhere, fixing her aim on Alina with her hands alone.

"..."

Splashing through a puddle, Alina stood in front of Vilfina.

Of course, she had not given up. Now that she didn't have Jade, she couldn't handle the dark gods in their twin form with that nasty regenerative ability, so she figured she had better odds trying to deal with the reject doll Vilfina.

But now the problem was *how* she would defeat Vilfina.

"Die." The giant woman fired, her arrow zooming at Alina. It moved too fast for the naked eye—Alina read the attack based on the movement of Vilfina's hands alone and dodged to the side. She wouldn't make it in time if she moved after Vilfina fired. And if she tried to block the attack, the arrow would hit her.

A puddle burst with a *bang* from the impact of the projectile, spraying droplets everywhere. It was so much more powerful than a mere arrow. Alina shivered anew, amazed that she had survived a hit from one of those things.

"I am Vilfina… Die…"

Alina used the same trick to dodge the next arrow Vilfina fired, and then it was nothing but dodging, with no chance to attack. The arrows were coming so fast that she would only put her life at even greater risk by getting closer.

But at this rate, I won't be able to win…!

With a squeak of her boot, she bounded off the rock face and went for Vilfina. The fixed distance she'd been keeping between them rapidly shrank.

It seemed like Vilfina wasn't capable of complex thought—she was abnormally strong and nothing else. That meant beating her was simple—she just had to overpower her.

Alina had just one idea as to how she could accomplish this.

Dodging the arrows that came at her one after another, Alina closed in on Vilfina in the blink of an eye. Now she was in deadly territory. If her focus broke for even an instant, if she overlooked a single move from Vilfina, her life would be snuffed out in an instant.

"I am Vilfina… Die."

Vilfina's arrow made a shrieking sound as it fired.

Alina let out a breath, putting all her strength into slamming the arrow of death head-on with her war hammer. The entire cave rumbled with a terrific *crack*.

How had Alina overpowered the dark god Silha?

Alina didn't know why she had beaten him, but there had clearly been some power at work. Even though they had been evenly matched at the beginning, Alina came out on top in the end.

A lower-ranked power could not beat a higher-ranked power. That was the only thing she was certain of when it came to the mysteries of skills.

So it made sense to her that two Dia skills, which were of the same rank, would be evenly matched when turned against each other. Put another way: Nothing more and nothing less could happen. The skills would remain equal in might, no matter what.

So then why had Alina possessed the strength to break through the dark god Silha's Dia skill? The only explanation Alina could think of was *the possibility that her skill was a rank higher in power than Dia skills.*

For example, perhaps Alina's *Dia Break* could transform into something beyond a Dia skill under certain conditions.

The arrow penetrated her war hammer, making a nasty grinding sound. But Alina continued to strain against it. The arrow of death dug into her war hammer, skimmed her shoulder, and flew away. At the same time, her damaged silver war hammer burst into white particles, which scattered and vanished.

"Ngh…!"

Blasted away by the force of the arrow, Alina rolled along the hard floor of the cave. The arrow had only grazed her, but it was enough to make the intense pain from earlier return. Sweat gushed from her whole body. But if she lost now, she would die, so she couldn't afford to focus on the pain right now.

"…Just so you know, I was *really* looking forward to the Centennial Festival, so I'm absolutely *furious* at having that interrupted…!" Alina hissed, clenching her teeth as she glared at Vilfina in front of her. "Every single time, you guys try to interrupt what little peace I have—do you think I'm just gonna let you get away with that…?!"

Alina thrust out her hand and yelled violently at the dark god. "Skill Activate: *Dia Break*!"

She didn't know what made her skill transform, so there was just one thing that she could do—keep fighting until that change occurred.

"Die…" Vilfina had been repeating the same thing over and over like a machine, but now her lips stopped flat. She went still as a statue as she looked at Alina, her hands freezing partway through nocking an arrow.

Because what had appeared in Alina's hands was not her usual silver war hammer.

It was a golden war hammer, wreathed in particles so bright they were dazzling to the eye.

"Die…die…" Vilfina was completely paralyzed—it was as if she was frightened of something. Instead, she fixed her previously empty gaze on Alina for the first time. There was undeniable fear reflected deep in her eyes.

"Die…!" Vilfina started to act strangely, in a different way from before. She aimed her arrow away from Alina—and pointed it at Lululee, who was collapsed on the ground.

"!"

"Die…" Vilfina drew her bow.

With a gasp, Alina bounded off the ground—but if Vilfina fired, it was over. And Alina would never catch up to the speed of that vicious arrow.

"Ngh…" Rushing, panicking, she raced desperately for Lululee. *But it's no use, I won't make it…*

Then suddenly, a completely baseless certainty rose in her heart, and she called his name: *"Jade!"*

That instant.

A large shield came slicing through the air in response, striking Vilfina's arm, throwing off the trajectory of her arrow just slightly. At almost the same moment, the arrow fired with a murderous whoosh through the air, destroying a spot a few steps ahead of Lululee.

But Alina didn't have the time to take that in; she changed

direction and went for Vilfina. Meanwhile, Vilfina was drawing her bow on her next target: Jade, who was sitting up on the ground.

"Don't you dare…!" Alina growled and leaped into the air. Scattering golden particles, she lifted her war hammer overhead.

"The one you're fighting…" Alina circled around in front of the arrow being fired. The arrow came zooming in at exactly the same moment as Alina's war hammer came swinging. Vilfina's killer arrow and Alina's war hammer crashed straight into each other.

"…is me!!"

There was a dull sound.

Alina's war hammer pushed through. She shattered the silver arrow with a fully body strike—and then the golden war hammer kept going, connecting with the deep black god core embedded in the base of Vilfina's neck.

"I'd been looking forward to it more than anything, and I toiled away at overtime… And after I was finally able to go to the Centennial Festival…I even turned that down to come here—do you understand why…?!"

With a *crrk crrk!* Alina's war hammer created countless tiny cracks in the god core, pulverizing it. Clenching her teeth, Alina wrung out an emotion somewhere between frustration and rage, flaring her eyes wide as she put force into her strike.

"I don't care if you're a dark god or a holy god…I'll never let you take away what I care about…!!"

Each time the war hammer sunk in further, Vilfina's shrieks and moans of anguish shook the cave, flinging water everywhere.

"Just die alreadyyyyyyyyyyy—!!"

At that moment, a crack decisively appeared in the god core with a *snap*…

"…Ah… Ahh…"

…Vilfina gave a weak gasp, turned to mist, and vanished.

44

Alina watched Vilfina disappear, then checked to see how Lululee was doing.

It only looked like she was passed out. The arrow wound on Alina's shoulder had disappeared completely now that she'd defeated Vilfina. After breathing a sigh of relief, she tried looking around the area again.

The mystical cave shone pale blue. The blue puddles of water sparkled, reflecting the light off the walls, and there lay a scene of carnage, blood splattered all over the place.

Alina was hit by a wave of exhaustion. She slung the unconscious Lululee over her shoulder, picking her rod up off the ground, and then, finally, went over to that lug.

"...So you're alive after all, huh? Not that I'm surprised," she said with exasperation to Jade, who was sprawled out on the ground below her.

"...But I can't get my arms or legs to work... It was a miracle I could throw my shield," he replied weakly.

Alina stuck her thumb up at him. "Nice toss."

"I was impressed you figured out I could still move, Alina."

"I just had the feeling you could. I mean, a guy with the tenacity of a cockroach like you just isn't the type to dead out after a cool line like '*I leave the rest to you.*'

"..."

Jade gave her a look of protest, which she ignored. After setting Lululee down, Alina practically fell into a sitting position, giving in to the exhaustion that weighed down on her whole body as she zoned out, staring into thin air. After a few moments of silence, with a dark sigh that blew away the aftertaste of victory, Alina muttered, "...In the end...I basically...wasn't able to enjoy the Centennial Festival..."

Her body was unsurprisingly heavy with exhaustion, and though

she wasn't entirely drained, she didn't have the energy left to go to the festival now. She had decided to enjoy the full day's schedule, but—she would be forced to give up on the first day.

"...Sorry..." For some reason, Jade hung his head like he was ashamed.

"Even if they are dark gods, they don't have to revive right in the middle of the Centennial Festival...!" Alina's voice trembled with frustration. She had decided that she would enjoy all three days of the Centennial Festival this year—she'd been preparing for it and fighting for it for so long. But for all her efforts, the festival had wound up getting attacked on the first day. And then a dark god had to go and get revived on top of that. What the heck? Was this some kind of divine punishment?

"Everyone is always trying to get in my way! What the heck...? What the heck?!" Alina wailed and broke down in tears.

45

"...It really is going on," Alina muttered in an almost-exasperated tone, as she watched the streets of Iffole bustling with festivalgoers as if this had been the plan all along. It was like the attack from a week ago was a dream or something.

It had already been one week since they'd defeated the dark gods. Though the Centennial Festival had restarted after the attack, the people in charge of it had held some cautious discussions about the resumption of the second and third days. In the end, it was decided that the Centennial Festival be temporarily put on hold, and a smaller scale, daylong festival would be held a week later.

I'm grateful they didn't just cancel the whole thing, she thought as she headed out for the Centennial Festival.

Despite the attack, the main street was packed with adventurers partying loudly like usual. After going to a street stall that she had failed to hit on the first day, Alina strolled along with a salt-grilled fish skewer in hand as she looked for her next target. That was when it happened.

Suddenly, she noticed everything around her come to a sharp halt. *This is…*

The adventurers tossing back booze, the loudly touting men at street stalls, the touchy-feely couples—they were all frozen as if time had stopped. No—it wasn't *as if* time had stopped.

"Hey, li'l miss."

To no surprise, Guildmaster Glen stepped out from the crowd of people, for whom time had actually stopped. This was the work of *Sigurth Chronos*.

The skill stopped time around the caster and enabled them to observe things. When Glen had been an adventurer in the field, this rare ability had been hailed as invincible, and it led him to become the strongest of his cohort, in both title and reality. But his skill didn't work on Alina because she had a Dia skill, which was of a higher rank than Sigurth skills. Alina and Glen were the only people who could move here right now.

"You helped us out again. So I came to give my thanks," he said.

"You didn't have to bother stopping time for something like that," Alina replied.

"It saves me a lot of trouble to do it like this."

"I guess you have a point…"

Alina was a receptionist, no more than a peon in the guild hierarchy—it would be a hassle if she were seen openly conversing with the guildmaster. People had already seen her going around the festival with Jade to begin with.

"Please tell Jade Scrade to exercise some of that consideration, too. He doesn't even care where he approaches me…"

"Ha-ha, it's no use telling him anything. That's definitely deliberate."

I knew it. I've got to teach him a lesson later…

"It sounds like you were up against a pretty tough enemy this time—or yet again, rather… Jade and Lululee were stuck in bed for a few days after you came back. The saving grace was that Lowe called for reinforcements, enabling us to carry them quickly from the Forest of Eternity to the healing room."

Kindness showing on his rugged, tanned face, Glen clapped a hand on Alina's shoulder and smiled. "Most of all, it's thanks to you that everyone was able to come back alive. You have my gratitude."

"It wasn't just thanks to me that we won this time, though… And wait, more importantly!" Alina furrowed her brows as she shot a nasty look at Glen, who was about two heads taller than her. "What happened to you promising to increase the number of receptionists at Iffole Counter and get rid of my overtime?!"

"Huh? H-hey, hold your horses. I've got a full plate, too."

"You'd better not go back on that…!" Alina growled, baring her teeth.

Glen recoiled a few steps, breaking into a cold sweat as he said, "W-well, this time I just came to thank you for defeating the dark god… Ah, I've got another appointment coming up, so I have to go."

"You'd better…you'd better…!"

"I—I get it, I get it. Enjoy the Centennial Festival, li'l miss!"

Glen tried to beat a hasty retreat, only to stop on a dime and turn back to Alina. "…By the way, li'l miss: I'll be counting on you next time, too."

"What?! Can you not say that?! It's bad luck!! There won't be a next time."

"Ha-ha, I guess so."

Glen played dumb and laughed, then slipped into the throng of frozen people. Eventually, he disappeared from view, and without a sound, time began moving again.

46

"Hmm. It's just about time for the main event."

The night was getting on, and the end of the Centennial Festival was fast approaching.

Likely because they'd gotten many adventurers requesting such, the condensed Centennial Festival completely skipped the program for the second day, covering only the events of the third.

People were saying that they just had to have the big event that was held every year on the third day—the soul's rest ceremony.

The soul's rest ceremony would bring the Centennial Festival to a close. Her heart filled with sadness over the fact that she didn't manage to hit every street stall and her stomach upset from all the grub, Alina emptied a wine-filled tankard as she gleefully headed to the main square.

Well, I wasn't able to fulfill my goal of enjoying the whole Centennial Festival, but I'm glad that the part I wanted to go to most, the soul's rest ceremony, is still happening.

But right as she was breathing a sigh of relief, the man she'd been hearing from far too often lately addressed her from behind. "Alina!"

" . . . "

A frown instantly formed on her face. Alina looked back over her shoulder, and there was Jade Scrade, waving one hand as he trotted up. He'd been literally covered in blood just a week ago, and now he was running up to her energetically—but she was used to that now. Jade raced over to her, grinning as he hit her with another nonsense proposal. "We only got halfway through our date on the first day, right? I figured we still had half left."

"Like hell we do! The first day was the first day, and that's over!" Alina huffed out an aggressive sigh, then suddenly went calm and looked away. "...Oh well. Come with me for a bit."

"Huh?" Despite having charged at her, Jade was taken aback, giving exactly two blinks. "Huh? I-is that okay, Alina…?"

"Uh-huh."

Taking Jade along with her, Alina headed for the big square. Going through the darkness of night to reach the piazza, which was enveloped in dazzling light, she bought a small bottle at a street stall by the entrance.

It had a small metal handle and was short and stout in shape. But this was no ordinary container. It was a light bottle, made using relic technology. A set amount of time after its production, it would vanish, leaving its contents behind. You might wonder what such a thing would be used for, and as it happened, it was exclusively used for the soul's rest ceremony. There was no question it had been developed for the sake of this day.

"This is…" Jade started to say something but didn't finish, walking at Alina's side.

The soul's rest ceremony was held on the third day of the Centennial Festival.

In mourning for the adventurers who died on the job, everyone put magic lights in special bottles and treated them like souls and placed them on a special stage—that was all the event was.

Already, hundreds of light bottles had been gathered at the central square, illuminating the place in a dim aggregate glow.

The cloth that had covered the special stage had now been removed. The fountain in the square had been decorated to look like a tree trunk, and the scaffolding for the light bottles stretched out from it like branches. From a distance, it looked just like a great tree made of light.

The water of the fountain was also sparkling from the glow of the light bottles, making the whole space look fantastical.

But this beautiful scene was ruined by its surroundings—the square was filled with adventurers sitting on the ground, drinking and partying, along with couples who were fooling around with each other. Not a single person was shedding tears in remembrance of the dead adventurers, but that wasn't at all a failure of their social obligations.

You didn't cry at the soul's rest ceremony—that had always been the unspoken rule. That way, the souls taking their journey to the heavens wouldn't be lonely—and those souls that remained could move on from their sadness.

"You can use magic, right, Jade?" With a sulky look, Alina shoved her empty bottle at Jade. "Put a light in it. I never studied magic, so I can't do it."

"…You don't mind?"

"Uh-uh."

Jade lit a light inside the bottle, and Alina placed it on the edge of the special stage. She bought a drink, then sat down on the stone paving of the square as she watched the special stage blaze bright from a distance.

"When I was little, an adventurer I knew died," Alina began.

"…Oh."

"That adventurer…his name was Shroud. We were pretty close."

"…"

After a strange pause, Jade muttered, "I see." He refrained from asking her questions. Alina wasn't going to say anything more, either. The two of them just gazed at the glow of the countless light bottles for a while, booze in hand.

"…Don't die, okay, Jade?" The words spilled from her lips of their own volition. After a few seconds of silence, Alina realized what she'd just gone and said and went red in the face, though she didn't know why. "W-well! You're about as tenacious as a cockroach, so I'm sure you wouldn't die even if someone tried to kill you! And anyway, it's got nothing to do with me whether you live or die! Forget what I said! Forget it!"

As Alina panicked and made an X with her arms, Jade smiled back at her sunnily.

"It's all right, Alina. I don't plan to die by anything but your war hammer."

"I said forget it…!" To hide her embarrassment, Alina splayed out on her back on the stone paving.

"Anyway, it turns out I wasn't able to enjoy the Centennial Festival this year, either!!" She shot up again to glug down booze from her tankard, then buried her face in her knees, back timidly rounded.

"In the end, I just went around the festival with you for the first day… Then that's just a date… There were lots of other nice-looking goods, lots of things I had my eye on, and I wanted to cover the whole festival, walking around eating over the course of three days…! Ahnn…hnn…wahhhhhhhhhhhh!!"

"C-calm down, Alina."

As Alina wailed, a voice cut through the crowds to address her.

"—Huh? Aren't you Alina from Iffole Counter?!"

A number of adventurer men surrounded Alina. They already reeked of alcohol, carrying tankards of liquor in one hand.

Here come the filthy bastards trying to pick her up. Jade muttered, glaring at the men. "Hey, you guys, if you're looking to pick up girls, go somewhere else. Alina's on a date with me right now."

"No way, it's Mr. Silver Sword?! Aww, man, you're all cozy with Jade? So you *do* like a pretty face after all, Alina!"

"That's not what's going on here." Alina, who had been bawling like a child until that moment, instantly flipped right back into work mode.

"He just gave me an offer I couldn't refuse to make me go on a date. This is like a new type of sugar dating."

"Hey, Alina, you're really going to destroy my reputation…"

"Listen, this girl is so good at her job!"

* * *

One of the adventurers happened to make that remark, and the atmosphere instantly changed.

"Huh?" Alina blinked in confusion.

The adventurers nodded one after another in front of her, and they started talking loudly.

"Duh, of course she is! She's always handling quests at twice the speed of the other receptionists."

"Though in exchange, if you try chatting with her for even a second about anything unrelated to quests, she'll kill ya with a glance! Ga-ha-ha! But she's fast at her job."

"She's always smiling, but for some reason, she's scary! But I still line up at her window. It's just kinda a habit—like it feels good to see her just getting right through it so fast."

"They make you wait so long at Iffole Counter, I never really liked to go before. But ever since Alina's shown up, I've started going."

"It's really nice to have her when things are busy."

"I've been watching her ever since she started out there. Back then, she always looked so desperate on the job, but at some point, she started being confident and capable. It makes me feel kinda glad but kinda sad."

Praise she hadn't even been expecting came from the adventurers' lips one after another.

"...Huh...?" Alina just watched them in a daze, mouth hanging half-open. She was speechless.

Beside her, Jade was smiling with satisfaction for some reason, as if he was the one getting complimented. "So they say, Alina. Isn't that nice?"

"N-nice...?" Flushing red for some reason, Alina looked away automatically.

She'd never even considered that the adventurers might be thinking such things—that they were grateful to her.

Since that was her job, she'd just been doing the obvious.

She'd started working as a receptionist for the income, for the stable lifestyle, so that she could go home on time. She had always been doing all that work for the sake of building her own ideal peace. Not once had she thought of doing something on behalf of the adventurers. But...

"No matter how crowded it is, y'see, she'll never refuse ya. Though she's got a scary look on her face, she'll take care of the line right through to the end, and she'll definitely get you your quest. Other places have no problem saying they're busy and sending you somewhere else..."

Even though they were a bunch of drunks, for some reason their comments made her chest heat up. Her heart was filled with a feeling she couldn't name. They warmed her core.

So much that it was hot.

Hot enough to burn right up...

Ahh, this was...

Anger.

"...I see... In other words...you were all deliberately lining up at my window and making overtime for me...?" Alina muttered very, very low.

Then Jade, who had been nodding in satisfaction at her side, startled and panicked. "Hoooooooold on, Alina. I think they were being nice..."

"I don't need pretty stories! All I want is to go home on time!!"

"Come on..."

"Making more damn work for me...! Clench your teeth for this, you adventurer scum!!" Alina yelled, slamming her empty tankard on the ground and making a fist as she huffed and swung at an adventurer.

"Hold up, hold up, Alina!" Jade quickly grabbed her hands, holding them behind her back to restrain her. She was too drunk to think to activate her skill—a coincidentally narrow escape for both her and the adventurers.

"Hey, hold on, Alina! Calm down! Don't be so rash!"

"Shaaaaaddap, you assholes—don't you dare target my reception window! When mine is crowded, march yourselves over to the other windows! All I want is to go home on schedule! Stop giving me more overtiiiiime!!!"

"Ohh, that's a girl with spunk! You wanna arm wrestle me?" The adventurer was actually enjoying being yelled at and rotated his shoulder.

Alina punched him in the face.

Immediately, cheers went up from all the drunks, and they stirred her up further, saying, "Nice, Alina! Do it again!"

Surrounded by the cheery adventurers, a low, resentful remark escaped from between Alina's clenched teeth. "Because of...because of that overtime...! I struggled so much trying to attend the Centennial Festival, which I'd been looking forward to all this time...! But then I couldn't even enjoy half of it...! What the heck, am I cursed?! Did I do something bad in a past life?!" By the last half of her statement, she was half sobbing, shoulders shaking and eyes watering.

She had been looking forward to the Centennial Festival more than anything this year, putting in so much effort at work and doing everything she could to participate. She felt so much more emotional about it than the people who took it for granted that they could attend, even if they took an afternoon nap.

"I understand how you feel, Alina. Let's enjoy it every year, for sure. Okay? Hey, you guys, Alina's feeling emotional right now, so go away, shoo."

"All right, guys! The third wheels are getting out!"

With Jade shooing them off, the adventurers yelled, "Get out, time to go!" weirdly energetic as they dispersed back into the nighttime festivities.

"Ahh! Jade, so this is where you were."

As Alina sniffled and hugged her knees, her face a mess from tears and snot, someone came up to replace the adventurers.

"Sending us out to buy stuff for you while you and Alina go on a date? That's not fair, leader."

It was Lululee and Lowe. They had both been walking around searching for Jade, and Lowe, who was carrying heavy paper bags in both arms, looked quite weary. Conversely, the shadow of depression that had been on Lululee's face lately was completely lifted. She looked cheerful, like a weight had been taken off her shoulders.

"Urk, you found us."

Lululee beamed at Alina and her panicking party leader. "This is perfect, Alina! Let's continue with the festival now!"

"...Huh?" Not having a clue what she meant, Alina sucked back her tears and blinked in puzzlement.

Seeing Alina like that, Lowe curled his lips in a smirk. "We bought everything the stalls hadn't sold before the festival ends. It's mostly leftovers, but I figure they'll let us savor the festival a little longer, right?"

"Let's go back to the inn and have a wild after-party!"

"After...after-party...?"

"Let's go, Alina."

As Alina just sat there with her mouth agape, Jade brought her to her feet. "We were talking about it together. Since we managed to defeat a dark god again and made it back home alive...we're gonna throw a party!"

Just then, Jade was interrupted by the grand ring of a trumpet from the band.

That was the announcement that it was midnight—the festival was over, and the soul's rest ceremony was kicking off.

The chattering adventurers all froze at the sound of the trumpet and looked at the center of the square, toward the special stage. And then after a brief moment of silence...

The light bottles melted away one after another, freeing the glowing orbs within.

"Ohh! There they go, Alina!"

Cheers went up all around them as the orbs began floating up into the sky; the sight they'd all been waiting for was here at last.

"Hmm, cheers...?!"

Since the soul's rest ceremony was for mourning the dead, Alina had imagined a more solemn affair. The cheers, which weren't much different from drunks yelling at a bar, startled her. When she hastily looked all around, a strange sight greeted her.

Encouraged by the noise and merrymaking, some people broke out into song; drunk men stripped naked; people tossed back booze without noticing that the light bottles had vanished; people whistled through their fingers; people got into fights and started punching at one another; it was really barbaric and raucous. The atmosphere was so thoroughly unglamorous that Alina wanted to rage and yell at everyone, *What the heck are you doing below these beautiful lights rising up into the sky one after another?*

"H-huh...?"

Alina's jaw dropped at the view. At the same time, she realized that the ceiling of lights of the soul's rest ceremony had seemed so beautiful to her when she first saw it two years ago because she'd been looking at it from afar.

"Isn't that nice, Alina? It's no overstatement to say that if you see this, you've experienced about half the Centennial Festival. In other words, you've managed to enjoy a hundred percent of the Centennial Festival this year." Jade tried to sum things up nice and pat.

"No way!!" Alina cut him off, snapping out of her daze clenching her teeth with a *nghhhh* as she pointed up at the bright sky. "Next year for sure...! Next year, I'll enjoy the entire Centennial Festival...! I swear on those lights...!"

"Alina, that's not what the soul's rest lights are for," Lululee pointed out.

"C'mon, who cares, right? Let's go to that after-party; my arms are sore...!!" Lowe griped.

And with their remarks following her, Alina started walking off to the guild inn for the after-party. The people who had gathered in the square to see the soul's rest ceremony all filtered off in different directions, too. Some were drawn toward the taverns, as if they had yet to drink enough—they were all a cheery lot.

This is...the soul's rest ceremony...

Nigh exasperated by the sight, which was nothing like she'd imagined, Alina began thinking dimly.

There was that light in the bottle that she'd been treating like Shroud's soul. Alina had always felt that his death was a tragic thing, so she had thought that if she mourned his soul during the soul's rest, something might change a little bit.

But maybe it's actually not that sad to begin with.

She'd been thinking that quite a lot lately.

Surely, if she had gone to soul's rest alone—forcing herself to go while drowning in overtime, watching those lights rise up alone—she would never have thought such a thing. She would have ruminated on her sorrows, recalled a vision of Shroud, and been properly solemn.

But the real thing was quite different. Between the friend who never left her side, and the adventurers who'd caused her overtime spouting off whatever suited them while laughing wildly, it had ended up being quite a raucous event.

It was annoying and pissed her off, and thanks to that, not only could she not be even a little solemn but she also didn't even have the time to feel sad.

Oh. So I'm not sad.

Just then, Alina turned around and looked up at the lights that were vanishing in the distant darkness of night.

At the end of the day, work was just work. It was nothing more and nothing less. Working for the sake of her lifestyle, going home on time for the sake of her peace and quiet—surely, those would continue to be Alina's greatest and most important goals—her ideals.

Yet it seemed that in becoming a receptionist, Alina had attained something besides life stability, a salary, and a large volume of overtime.

Maybe being with someone isn't so bad.

As that thought struck her, she relaxed her lips into the slightest of smiles.

The End

Afterword

Hello. It's been a long time. This is Mato Kousaka.

This series made adult readers uncomfortable in the first volume thanks to its vivid depictions of working extra hours—so how was Volume 2? I drew on my own experiences to include other common experiences of the workplace and overtime.

Oh, and some of the things in this volume really do happen in real life! Just like with Alina and the Centennial Festival, it's always when you've been looking forward to something for months that your superior forces work on you out of nowhere! Overtime surges in! And you come in on your days off! The timing is so awful, it's like it's intentional. "Damn you bossss!" you howl with rage on the inside as you accept your work with a smile. *Nghhhh...*

It goes without saying that Volume 2 is packed full of those feelings of resentment. It makes me wonder, do reality and society really never go the way you want...? But writing Alina allowed me to let go of the resentment I felt in those days. Isn't it nice you got to go to the festival, Alina?

My complaints aside, Lululee worked hard this time around.

I think those who have already read the book will have picked up on this, but this series setting is based on video games, specifically the type where there are job classes.

This may be weird to say when I'm writing a book about a girl who is a pure physical attacker who whacks things, but I am in fact someone with a tendency to pick the healer class. As for why, well, to be frank, it's because I want to heal my party and save them from trouble and have them thank me for it (I'm a dirty person full of ulterior motives).

But if you actually try being a healer, you'll discover that saving your party from trouble is really hard. Not only do you need to be familiar with the boss's attack patterns, but you also have to imagine what sort of dangers will arise based on your allies' equipment and movesets, and make preparations beforehand. Otherwise, you won't have an easy time getting your allies out of jams. If you're up against a tough boss, the party falls apart immediately, and it's game over.

That's what makes being a healer interesting! Using all your knowledge and experience (and an immense amount of time and money), you heal your allies at any cost, and when your party starts to fall apart, you get them back on their feet at any cost. It's an obsession at this point. Once you have that pride as a healer, the profession will have you fighting with blazing eyes. I tried shining a spotlight on that sort of healer in this book. I hope you enjoyed it.

Now then, for this book, I have to thank my editors Yoshioka and Yamaguchi, whom I heavily relied on; to Gaou, who has drawn some more incredibly cute illustrations for this book; to everyone from the editing department who has printed and advertised Volume 2; and most of all, to you, who have picked up Volume 2 of *Guild Receptionist*: I thank you from the bottom of my heart. Reality won't go like you want, but let's live on and work hard again tomorrow!

HAVE YOU BEEN TURNED ON TO LIGHT NOVELS YET?

86—EIGHTY-SIX, VOL. 1–12

In truth, there is no such thing as a bloodless war. Beyond the fortified walls protecting the eighty-five Republic Sectors lies the "nonexistent" Eighty-Sixth Sector. The young men and women of this forsaken land are branded the Eighty-Six and, stripped of their humanity, pilot "unmanned" weapons into battle...

Manga adaptation available now!

WOLF & PARCHMENT, VOL. 1–7

The young man Col dreams of one day joining the holy clergy and departs on a journey from the bathhouse, Spice and Wolf. Winfiel Kingdom's prince has invited him to help correct the sins of the Church. But as his travels begin, Col discovers in his luggage a young girl with a wolf's ears and tail named Myuri, who stowed away for the ride!

Manga adaptation available now!

SOLO LEVELING, VOL. 1–8

E-rank hunter Jinwoo Sung has no money, no talent, and no prospects to speak of—and apparently, no luck, either! When he enters a hidden double dungeon one fateful day, he's abandoned by his party and left to die at the hands of some of the most horrific monsters he's ever encountered.

Comic adaptation available now!